MW01042335

# A Woman's Revenge

Tiffany L. Warren
Sherri Lewis
Rhonda McKnight

## 3SISTERS BOOKS

"Inspiring readers...one book at a time."

**www.3sistersbooks.com**

First Printing May 2010
10 9 8 7 6 5 4 3 2 1

Printed in the United States of America

*This is a work of fiction. Any references or similarities to actual
events, real people, living or dead, or to real locales are intended
to give the novel a sense of reality. Any similarity in other names,
characters, places, and incidents is entirely coincidental.*

Submit Wholesale Orders to:

3 Sisters Books
4919 Flat Shoals Parkway, Suite 107B-187
Decatur, Georgia 30034
Email: contact.3sistersbooks@gmail.com

# Contents

# *one*

N adine stood in the foyer of Pascal's restaurant, breathing deeply and appreciating the aromas wafting over from the Sunday Brunch buffet. She closed her eyes and allowed herself to image the delectable taste of the juicy, golden fried chicken. Her tongue ran over her lips at the mere thought of the homemade macaroni and cheese. Her entire body shuddered with anticipation of the syrupy sweet candied yams.

She hugged herself and said a prayer; felt her food lust subside.

One glance at herself in the mirror to her right made Nadine smile. She admired her svelte figure in the clingy dress – something she'd never worn two years ago. Nadine's smile widened as she noticed a fine brother appreciate her with a double take, especially since he was with his wife.

She whispered, "Nothing tastes as good as skinny feels."

Nadine scanned the restaurant searching for her best friend Angelique. They hadn't seen each other in a year – since before Nadine's gastric bypass surgery.

When Nadine had decided that enough was enough and that her true love Jamal would never marry her in her three hundred pound body, she made the decision to have the surgery. She hadn't run it by her parents, sister or friends – especially Angelique and Jamal. She hadn't even prayed about it because she hadn't wanted to hear God tell her no.

She had the procedure done at a clinic in Boulder, Colorado. It was nearly fifteen hundred miles from her condo in Lithonia, GA. Too far away for anyone to come looking for her and too far for her to run if the going got tough.

And the going had gotten tough.

Her cover story was that she was enrolling in an accelerated Doctorate program. She'd told everyone that she'd found an excellent program and with the credits she'd already earned she would end up with a PhD in Higher Education Administration. It was a boring ruse for the most daring decision she'd ever made in her life and since she was typically a boring woman – everyone believed it.

She remembered how Jamal had responded when she'd told him she was leaving for a year.

She'd said, "It will be good for my career. I'll be able to run a community college when I'm done, or implement a program at our church."

"Deenie," he'd replied with a smile, "you should do whatever it is that God has for you. I'm sure you'll do well."

He hadn't said that he'd miss her, hadn't begged her to stay. He'd given a response that a man would give to his little sister on her way off to school for the first time.

But all of that would change now. He'd see her in her new body and suddenly realize all of the feelings that he'd suppressed.

She hoped.

Finally, Nadine spotted Angelique, sitting at a table near the window. She should've known. Angelique always wanted to gaze outdoors and people watch while she was eating.

Nadine let out a long breath, threw her shoulders back and strode across the room. She'd studied Miss Jay's walking classes on *America's Next Top Model* and liked to think that she had perfected a runway walk. It was a confident stride. The kind of walk that women put on when they knew men were watching.

She stopped short of the table and called out, "Angel!"

Angelique looked up, and the confusion in her eyes made Nadine's heart swell. Her own very best friend didn't even recognize her!

"Nadine?" Angelique asked as she rose from her seat.

Nadine nodded and tears burst from her eyes. "Yes, it's me!"

Angelique squealed and surrounded Nadine with a bear-hugged embrace. "Oh my God! Nadine, I don't believe this!"

Angelique hadn't changed at all in the year they'd been apart. She was still perfect. Her flawless hair barely even moved as she hugged Nadine and her perfect curves filled out a stunning cream pantsuit.

"You skinny heifer," Angelique said. "I think you might be smaller than me."

Nadine grinned. She was, in fact, smaller than Angelique. She never thought she'd see the day.

"What did your mother say when she saw you?" Angelique asked.

"She hasn't seen me yet. You're the first."

There was a reason Nadine had chosen to see Angelique before her parents. Her mother Joan, and her father Grant were severely obese, and they didn't see a problem with it at all. Nadine knew that as soon as her mother took one look at her, she was going to start baking.

Her parents were the ones who raised Nadine and her brother and sister on three hot meals a day, plus countless snacks in between. If one of her children said they were thirsty, Joan Robinson gave them sweet tea, not water. If they were sad, she offered words of encouragement wrapped up in a pasta dish.

Joan's favorite expression was, "Put some food on it." She believed that all wounds, internal and external, could be bandaged with food.

Nadine remembered her mother assuring her that she would find a man to love her and that it wouldn't be hard. She always told her that there were men in the world who liked a woman with "a little extra softness."

Joan would never understand why Nadine had gone through so much drama to lose weight. It was going to be an ordeal when she finally did see her parents.

"Wait until I tell Jamal!" Angelique exclaimed. "He's going to be thrilled to pieces."

Wait until *she* told Jamal?

Before Nadine could fix her mouth to object, Angelique had whipped out her cell phone. It mildly annoyed Nadine that Angelique only pressed one button to dial Jamal. Why would she have him on speed dial?

Nadine wasn't sure if it was the ringing of the phone or the ringing in her ears that made her want to jump up from the table and run.

"Hey baby, it's me," Angelique said into the phone.

Nadine's breath caught in her throat and her stomach churned. The room spun around as if she'd had too much wine. Angelique was calling Jamal *baby.* That could only mean one thing.

She should've run when she'd had the chance.

"You're not going to believe this. Nadine has lost a lot of weight! Yes....Like a whole person!"

Angelique put her hand over the phone and smiled at Nadine. "He said, Praise God!"

Then she went back to the phone call. "She'll look great in a bridesmaid gown now...Well you know what I mean. When we finally do get married."

Unable to maintain her decorum any longer, Nadine rose to her feet.

"You okay, Nadine?" Angelique asked, with a true look of concern on her face.

"Y-yes. I just need food. Let's eat. Talk to Jamal later."

Nadine scurried away from the table with Angelique following at her heels. Nadine tried to breathe, but it was as if Angelique was stealing her oxygen. Just like she'd stolen her man.

"So...are you surprised that Jamal and I are tying the knot?" Angelique asked.

Nadine stopped cold in front of the meat display. Surprised? Surprised was not the word she was looking for. The words she wanted to use couldn't even cross her lips. Not after she'd gotten that cussing demon cast out a few years ago.

"I didn't know you were interested in Jamal," Nadine stated.

Angelique burst into laughter. "Are you kidding me? I've always been interested in Jamal. It's just that it was always the three of us, so we never got a chance to connect on that level."

"The three of us?"

"You know what I mean! We'd go bowling together and to the movies together."

Nadine replied "We were part of the single's ministry. Those were ministry outings, not dates."

"Right! But I just said that to say that I've always wanted to get to know Jamal better. I just wasn't able to until you were gone. It almost seemed natural that we'd turn to one another, when we both missed you so much."

Nadine dropped the plate she was holding and it crashed to the floor causing people at the buffet to look in her direction. She didn't care that everyone was looking at her, though, because all of her attention was on her man-stealing whore of a best friend.

Angelique flagged down a restaurant employee. "We've had a bit of an accident here."

Yes, there had been an accident. Nadine had accidentally left the love of her life with a barracuda.

"When I went away, Jamal pursued a relationship with you?" Nadine asked.

She needed to hear that this was Jamal's doing. That was the only way she could imagine salvaging their friendship. Because Angelique *knew* how she felt about Jamal.

Angelique giggled. "Well, he needed a bit of help. You know Jamal. It was almost like it never occurred to him that we could be an item, but we've been together for six months now."

*I wonder why?* Nadine took another plate from the stack next to the buffet and stared at all of the food that she wouldn't be able to eat. Her gastric bypass only allowed her to take a few bites of anything. She wouldn't be able to put food on this wound.

"Anyway, you're in the wedding of course. Maid of honor," Angelique said.

"Of course."

Nadine heard herself responding to the most ludicrous of requests. How dare Angelique act as if she was oblivious to Nadine's feelings about Jamal? Nadine wanted to get real ghetto with it, pull her to the floor and scratch her eyes out. But here she was saying yes to being the maid of honor in her wedding.

"How did he propose?" Nadine asked.

Nadine had always dreamed of Jamal doing something spectacular and romantic when it was time for him to propose to her.

"Well, he didn't actually propose," Angelique explained. "One day I introduced him to a friend as my fiancée and he didn't object. We've been engaged since then. We've been talking about marriage for a while though. You know how Jamal wants to wait until marriage and everything to get the cookie. So it's only a matter of time."

Nadine fingered the ring on her right ring finger that symbolized her vow of celibacy. Nadine and all of the core members of the singles ministry – Jamal and Angelique included - had taken the vow together. They'd all promised to save themselves for the mate God had purposed or to serve as a vessel for God.

Not all of the singles meant it when they'd taken the vow, but *she* had meant it. And so had Jamal. It made her feel a little better to know that he was keeping his vow. Angelique hadn't made him forget his promise to God, so maybe he hadn't forgotten the close bonds of their friendship.

Perhaps there was still time for her to win him back. Nadine took one glance at the confident Angelique and knew that this would be the fight of her life.

# two

After brunch with Angelique Nadine went home to her condo with a lot on her mind. She knew she had to make a move, but what? It was hard for Nadine to plot her comeback, though, because her younger sister/house sitter, Carly, was still in her condo refusing to go back home to their parents' house.

Nadine plopped down on her cream leather sofa, the one Jamal had helped her pick out, and let out a long sigh. Carly was watching television and eating ice cream – her two most favorite pastimes.

Nadine knocked Carly's feet from her glass and marble coffee table. She remembered Jamal carrying the heavy table up two flights of stairs all because Nadine had forgotten to schedule a delivery, and she wanted it the very day she moved in.

Carly being there in her space while she fantasized about a life with Jamal was annoying. Nadine wanted her little sister gone, so that she could wallow in solo misery.

"Carly, when exactly are you gonna start packing?"

"What do you mean packing?" Carly asked. "This is where I live!"

Nadine crossed her arms and slumped back into the couch cushions. Carly wasn't getting the point. "I mean getting your stuff and moving back to Mama and Daddy's house."

"Well I was thinking that you've got three bedrooms..."

"And I'm just supposed to let you live here for free?" Nadine's furrowed brows should've told Carly the answer to that question.

"I did take care of your place for you! A whole year and you didn't visit once. Not even a holiday. You didn't half call anybody! Now you trying to kick me to the curb."

It wasn't just her sister that Nadine hadn't called. She was ashamed to admit that she didn't have the strength, willpower and conviction to lose the weight on her own. Nadine also hated lying to everyone. She was a horrible liar, and every time she made a call home from the weight loss clinic, she had to retell the story she'd concocted.

Nearly a whole year had gone by without her hearing Jamal's voice. It was torture, but the thought of hearing him declare his love had been the motivation she'd needed.

Nadine had wanted to do a big reveal of her weight loss after her year of dieting, exercising and weight lifting was completed. Now, she was regretting that. She'd been gone too long.

"I had to get myself together."

Carly got up from the couch, and placed her bowl in the sink. She didn't wash it. Typical. "Well, Mama is still mad at you for that," Carly declared in her know-it-all little sister tone.

*I wonder if Jamal was angry too.* Nadine's thoughts wandered away from her sister's conversation and back.

"Mama's just gonna have to be mad."

"She's gonna be even madder when she sees how skinny you are. You can't avoid going over there forever."

Nadine sighed. The thought of seeing her parents was stress inducing. Back in the day, she would've eaten eat half a row of Oreos to deal. Now, she was cured of that particular demon. "I know, I know. But Mama should be happy for me."

"Why? Because you got half your stomach and intestines ripped out?" Carly gave Nadine a disgusted look, as she grabbed a bag of potato chips off the kitchen counter and ate a handful. "Girl, I woulda just stayed big."

Nadine made a mental note to clear all of the junk food out of her house. Carly was just gonna have to get her junk food fix elsewhere.

"That's you. Besides, that's not how the surgery works."

Carly pursed her lips together and narrowed her eyes in a knowing glare. "I know why you did it too."

"Because I want to be healthy?"

Carly laughed out loud. "You might want to be healthy, but you also want a man. A man named Jamal."

Nadine marched up to Carly, took the bag of chips out of her hand and rolled it shut. Carly had eaten enough. "Maybe that was part of it, but it doesn't mean anything now. He's marrying Angelique."

"That white girl? Ain't that about a mutha. You go off for a year, getting skinny for this brotha and he runs off with a white chick?" Carly wiped the grease from the chips onto her jeans with an exaggerated flair.

"Tell me about it," Nadine complained. "My thing is that Angelique knows how much I care for Jamal."

"He knows too," Carly said.

"I've never shared my feelings with him!"

"Girl, please. The whole world knows that you are in love with him, including Jamal. He just acted like he didn't know."

Nadine opened the bag of chips in her hand and ate one without thinking. Could it be true? Could Jamal have known about her feelings? If he did, then he was at fault too.

"So what are you gonna do about it?" Carly asked.

"I'm going to be the maid of honor in their wedding, I suppose."

"That's fat Nadine talking. Skinny Nadine needs to make it do what it do."

Nadine rolled her eyes. "What do you even mean?"

"Get. Your. Man." Carly did a little booty bounce to emphasize each word. She reminded Nadine of Mo'Nique doing a Beyonce routine.

Nadine walked around the still dancing Carly and sat back down on the couch. "How am I supposed to do that?"

"Duh! You take him back."

"Take him? I can't take anyone from Angel. She's gorgeous and smart and..."

Carly sat next to Nadine and gave her the hand. "First of all, you're gonna stop calling that girl Angel. An angel is sweet. She stole your man. And, I don't know if you noticed, but you're gorgeous too."

"But what if Jamal looks at me and still sees a big girl?"

This, to Nadine, was a valid concern. She even looked at herself sometimes and remembered where the rolls and crevices had once resided. It was one of the things that kept her from veering off her fitness path.

"You were gorgeous then too!" Carly fussed. "So what if that's what he remembers?"

"Do you really think I can take him from Angelique?"

"Does Beyonce wear weave?"

Nadine pondered the possibility. Did she really have what it took to be a man stealer? What if it wasn't her size that had kept her from a romance with Jamal? What if it was her personality? What if he just wasn't feeling her?

"How do you suggest I begin?" Nadine asked her street-wise sister.

"If I tell you, can you please stop trying to kick me out of your crib?"

Nadine cocked her head to one side and sucked her teeth like she used to do when she argued with Carly as a girl. She knocked Carly's feet off the coffee table once more.

"I guess you can stay if you keep your rusty dogs off my furniture."

"Don't worry big sis. I'll make sure to be ghost if you have any spend-the-night company. I know y'all saved folk like to get down too."

"Humph! Not me. I won't be getting down until I get a ring.

Carly cracked her neck back and forth like she was Beyonce and sang a few lines from "Single Ladies".

Nadine joined in and the jumped up and tried to do the choreography from the video.

The two sisters burst into laughter at their antics. Nadine imagined Jamal putting a ring on her finger and sighed. What once seemed like the inevitable end of her weight loss journey now seemed like a fantasy.

"Well, we can't even talk about rings yet. Let's focus on getting the man," Nadine stated. "What do I do? Just go up to him and tell him how much I love him?"

"Girl, stop! Do I have to teach you everything? He's going to tell *you* how much he loves you."

"Yeah, right."

"You gotta believe you can do this, Nadine. First thing, you've got to make him break it off with Angelique."

"Make him break it off? I don't know how to do that."

"Think about it. You're her best friend. Every girl has secrets that she'd never tell her man but that she'd tell her girlfriend."

"Secrets."

"Yes, secrets. And if she doesn't have any juicy ones, then we can invent them if we have to."

"You want me to make something up?"

"Does Gary Coleman wear lifts in his shoes? Girl, yeah."

Nadine couldn't see herself inventing anything, but after the long hard year she'd spent starving herself to get her new body, anything was possible.

# *three*

N adine took in a big gulp of air before she and Carly walked through the door of their parents' house. It was like stepping into a time machine. Nothing had changed since she and her siblings were children.

Nadine's mother, Joan, had a one-theme decorating style. And that one theme was food. There were paintings of fruit, people dining and a woman frying chicken in an old-fashioned kitchen. The vases and bowls that adorned the tables and counters were not filled with pretty rocks or decorative potpourri. They were filled with miniature candy bars.

Nadine sent up a prayer of self control. It was as if she could smell the chocolate through the candy wrappers. She even thought she heard the candy calling her name.

Joan hurried to the door, still wearing her cooking apron. She stopped cold when she saw Nadine. Carly let out a little giggle and kissed her mother on the cheek. "Hey, Mama."

Joan did not reply to Carly. She was too busy working herself into a nervous state looking at her other daughter. Her newly svelte daughter.

"Lord, help," She cried in her prayers-of-the-righteous voice.

"Mama..."

Nadine had waited until the Monday evening following her brunch with Angelique to reveal her weight loss to her parents. It seemed she hadn't waited long enough.

Joan stumbled through the living room and into the dining room, holding one hand to her head in true dramatic fashion. She plopped down into one of the dining room chairs, chest heaving in and out. She was close to hyperventilating.

Nadine followed her mother into the dining room and sat next to her at the table. "Mama, calm down."

The table was full of food. It looked like an all-you-can-eat buffet. There was fried chicken, fried pork chops, macaroni and cheese, greens, candied yams, potato salad, red beans and seasoned rice, biscuits and gravy. Nadine's stomach lurched as the smells assaulted her nose and made their way down to her cramping stomach. It was way too much food for five people, but by the time her family was done eating dinner, there would be very little left over.

"Rob, bring me some sweet tea!" Joan cried. "I think my blood sugar is low."

Nadine's brother Rob shared a smile with her. They had always laughed at their mother's theatrics behind her back. They all normally stayed quiet and indulged Joan until she calmed down and her blood sugar normalized. No medical doctor had actually ever told Joan that she'd had low blood sugar, but since that was her excuse for every tirade, her children played along.

"Why'd you do it, Deenie?" Mama Joan asked. "You were fine the way you were."

"I was over three hundred pounds."

"And you were happy and full. Now you can't even eat a sandwich without getting sick." Rob handed her a glass of tea. "Thank you, baby."

It was true that Nadine could no longer overeat or drown her sorrows in food like she used to. It was part of the price she was willing to pay to finally have Jamal in her life for good. He was worth all of the biscuits, chocolate, cupcakes and croissants.

Nadine's stomach grumbled at the thought of her favorite things.

Daddy Grant waddled into the room and took his normal seat at the head of the table. He could barely walk anymore without his knees giving out. It saddened Nadine that her daddy had eaten himself into a cripple. Soon, he'd need a scooter to get across the room.

"Your mother's right, Nadine," Daddy Grant said. You know once them doctors slice you open they gonna have to keep cuttin' on ya'."

"Daddy, I'm healthier than I've ever been."

"You look sickly," Grant replied.

"Anemic," Joan added.

Carly asked, "Can one of y'all saved people please say grace so we can eat? I like to have my chicken while it's still hot."

Grant bowed his head and closed his eyes. His family followed suit. "Thank you Lord for bringing Nadine back safe, Lord, even if she ain't in one piece. Even if only half of her returned. I pray that you bless this food and cause it to be nourishment and strength to Nadine's body in particular. God, I pray that you heal her from this bulimarexia demon that seemed to grab hold to her. By your stripes we are healed, so I claim victory in the blood of Jesus. Lord I love you, Lord I thank ya'."

Everybody at the table said 'amen' except Nadine. She rolled her eyes and said her own prayer.

The bowls and dishes were passed quickly as huge portions of everything was served onto super-sized plates. Nadine took a chicken wing, a spoonful of greens and a spoonful of red beans.

"Please tell me you're eating more than that," Joan said.

"Mama, I can't eat anymore than that. My stomach won't hold it."

"No wonder you look like a skeleton then. They had more dinner than that in the concentration camps."

"Well, I think you look good, Deenie." Nadine's brother Robert gave her a hug. "You're inspiring me to get healthy." This he said while he added three biscuits to his plate from the bowl on the table.

Nadine gave her brother a sad smile. "Thanks Rob."

"Well, I hope you don't get your stomach cut out too, Rob! I need y'all to take care of me in my old age."

"Stop being melodramatic, Mama," Carly said. "Besides I'm not getting cut or losing a pound. I love being big and sexy."

"The blood of Jesus!" Joan hollered. "You need to stop with all that sexy talk and you ain't got husband the first. God don't like ugly."

"Oh please, mama! You've never felt big and sexy? I feel sorry for Daddy then," Carly teased from her seat at the table.

"Y'all mama is plenty sexy," Grant said with pride.

"I will not stand for this dirty talk at my dinner table."

Carly laughed out loud and then whispered, "Sexy..."

Mama Joan slammed her fork down on the table. "For goodness sakes. Pass me that macaroni and cheese. Nadine tell me about your friend Angelique. Carly says she's getting married."

"She's dating Jamal."

Nadine could barely fix her mouth to say the words without feeling sick. And she wanted to strangle Carly for telling their mother about it.

"Isn't that your fella?" Grant asked.

"He's my friend, Daddy."

Grant frowned. "You was sho'nuff in love with him. I thought he was sweet on you too, all them flowers he used to buy for you."

Nadine smiled wistfully at the memory of the flowers. It was calla lilies that her father remembered. She and Jamal had a little tradition going where they'd share one another's successes by purchasing each other's favorite things. Nadine had told Jamal that her favorite thing was lilies because she thought it sounded fat and greedy to admit that her true favorite thing was chocolate.

When Jamal had a success, she bought him one of those two dollar Matchbox cars. After every sermon he preached, Nadine presented him with a different minia-ture luxury car. Tears threatened to sting her eyes as she silently reflected on the time she'd spent picking out those cars.

The gifts were their secret friend code. Nadine's heart ached to see Jamal and tell him how much those trifles had meant to her.

"It's fine Daddy," Carly said. "Nadine's fella maybe forgot about her, but she's back now. New and improved."

"Humph," Daddy grunted. "If he didn't want you when you were big, maybe he's not the one."

Nadine looked down at the sparse contents of her plate. She wondered if there was any truth to her father's words. Could God have someone else for her?

No. That couldn't be true. Nadine had prayed night after night to have Jamal as her husband. She had named and claimed him under the blood. He was hers and no one was going to steal their destiny.

Not even her best friend.

# four

Nadine watched intently as Jamal stepped through the doors of the busy Starbucks. He held the door for two pretty young women, and they both gave him a second look. One of them slipped him her card that he graciously accepted and placed in his sport coat jacket.

As he swaggered over to her table, Nadine drank him in like a man dying of thirst would lap a tall glass of lemonade. His caramel brown, sun-kissed skin glistened, his low haircut was trimmed to perfection and his dress shirt struggled to camouflage his muscular physique.

He held in his hand a bouquet of peach colored lilies, tinged with a hint of pink.

Nadine exhaled wistfully. *If only he were mine.*

It had taken a small miracle for Nadine to plan a one-on-one meeting with Jamal. Every lunch and dinner suggestion had been met with an alternative set of plans by Angelique. It was as if Angelique instinctively knew what Nadine was up to.

Angelique had graciously offered that they could all do something together, and Nadine had accepted. If they all spent time together, it would only help her plan. But the only way she was going to win Jamal back was to get him away from his fiancée, so she'd settled for afternoon coffee.

"Deenie," Jamal said as he approached the table. "You look amazing."

The breathless way that he said her name caused Nadine's heart to flutter. She stood from the table so that he could get the full view. She'd worn a cream wrap around dress and orange leather sling backs. A chunky yet simple necklace glistened right above her cleavage, inviting Jamal to take a gander. She thought that the look was sexy, and apparently Jamal did too from the way he was gawking at her.

Jamal lifted Nadine from the floor in a man-sized embrace. She couldn't remember him ever attempting that before, or even really hugging her. She could only remember the one-armed, brotherly, church hugs that he was fond of giving all the women in church – from the mother's board down to the youth ministry.

This was a grown and sexy hug.

There was silence for a few moments when they sat down. Nadine floundered for something to say, but Jamal seemed to enjoy the absence of sound. He stared at Nadine so intensely, that she pulled at her dress to hide the display of bronzed cleavage.

"I'm gonna go and get my coffee," Jamal said. "Don't go anywhere pretty lady."

Against her will, Nadine blushed. "I'm not going anywhere."

She watched him walk away from the table, and this view was just as intriguing. He'd been working out, and his broad shoulders looked so manly that Nadine had to avert her eyes and look away. She rebuked herself for thinking of him with no shirt.

A smile graced his face as he returned with his drink. A venti Cafe Mocha. Nadine didn't even have to ask. She knew it was his favorite.

"I take it you didn't go to Colorado to study," Jamal said as he sat back down at the table.

"I didn't. But I couldn't tell you I was going to a weight loss clinic for a year. You'd think I was crazy."

Jamal took both her hands and said, "I wouldn't think you were crazy. I'd want to know how your bills were getting paid, but I wouldn't think you were crazy."

Nadine laughed out loud. Jamal was so practical. The first thing he thought of with her being gone for a year was her bills!

"I saved for the adventure, Jamal. My credit is intact, and my teaching job is waiting for me in the fall."

He wiped imaginary sweat from his brow. "Whew! In that case, congratulations."

"I should be congratulating you on your engagement."

"Thank you."

Nadine's heart sank with disappointment. She'd wanted to hear him deny being engaged to Angelique. She'd wanted to hear him say that it was something Angelique had concocted in her own imagination.

"That's all? Am I not entitled to details?" Nadine tried to hold together her façade of joy at Angelique's and Jamal's relationship, but it was difficult when he didn't show any excitement at all.

"There really isn't much to tell. We started dating a little while after you left. We're not officially engaged, but

Angelique keeps telling everyone that we are, so I guess I'll go along with it."

Nadine wanted to ask him if he loved Angelique, but it seemed much too early in the conversation for that.

"You'll go along with it?" she asked instead. "Aren't you happy about it?"

Jamal took a long pause before answering. "I am. I feel that it's the will of God. It just happened so quickly, I guess I'm still adjusting to the idea."

It had taken him too long to answer that question, and the pause gave Nadine hope.

Nadine sipped her venti, sugar-free, soy chai latte. "Have you always had feelings for her? She claims that it didn't happen sooner because I was always in the way."

Jamal's brow line furrowed into an intense frown. "You weren't in the way."

"Maybe I was," Nadine offered with a nonchalant shrug. "It seems you found each other as soon as I was out of the picture."

This seemed to make Jamal uncomfortable. He shifted in his seat and sipped his coffee.

"Let's talk about you," Jamal said changing the subject. "What made you finally decide to lose weight?"

Nadine's eyes widened. She hadn't prepared a cover story for her weight loss. Her original plan was to tell Jamal that she'd done it all for him, so that he'd look at her and want her in the way a man wants a woman. But that was before she found out about him and Angelique. She couldn't tell him that *now*.

"It was time," she said.

"Why didn't you call while you were gone? I missed you, and I don't know, maybe I could've offered some encouragement."

Nadine's heart fluttered. He'd *missed* her? Then the fluttering stopped. He hadn't missed her that much, because he'd had Angelique to keep him company.

"I missed you too. Angelique too. But I couldn't keep lying. You would've asked me about my classes, and I would've had to tell another lie. It was easier that way."

Jamal covered Nadine's hand with his own. "If you say so. But it wasn't easy for me. I needed my favorite cheerleader."

"Wouldn't that be Angelique now?"

Jamal snatched his hand away and took another sip of his coffee. "Do you think your life is going to change now that you're thin?"

"I don't know. What do you think?"

Jamal grinned. "I suspect you're going to have a lot of suitors. I can think of a few brothers at Greater Bethany that are gonna be knocking down your door to get a date."

Nadine sipped her latte again to avoid blurting out the words that were caught in her throat. *I don't want anyone but you!*

"So," Nadine said after composing herself. "Since I'm the maid of honor in your wedding, I'd like to plan an engagement party."

There. The words were out and she couldn't take them back. Step one of her plan had been activated.

"An engagement party?"

"Yes, it'll be just the extended family at a dinner. But don't tell Angel. I want it to be a surprise! A gift from her best friend."

Jamal replied, "Well, I have never met anyone in her family outside of her parents, so that sounds good. Meeting the family is important, right?"

"I couldn't agree with you more."

# five

J amal paced back and forth across his living room carpet. He couldn't sit still after meeting Nadine for coffee; his mind was a jumble of thoughts and his heart a potpourri of emotion.

Nadine was back. She was gorgeous. And his feelings for her hadn't died when she left town.

He remembered how he felt a year ago when she'd announced her plan. He had taken her out to dinner under the guise of celebrating the launch of his evangelism ministry, but he really had planned to spill the contents of his heart and tell her of the secret he'd been holding within.

He was falling in love with Nadine.

But when she said that she'd be gone – indefinitely at that – Jamal rethought his revelation. Was it a sign from God that He didn't want them to be together?

He'd sent Nadine on her way, with his best wishes and prayers. She hadn't called, emailed, written letters or anything resembling communication. Nadine had shut herself off from the world and from their friendship. Jamal had tried to understand, but without word from Nadine, it was hard to make heads or tails of her disappearing act.

Dating Angelique had come about almost organically. Because of Nadine, they all served on the same committees and ministries – a Three Musketeer type friendship. But with Nadine gone, hormones had kicked into gear. The physical attraction between he and Angelique had become impossible to ignore, and since they were already friends, a relationship was a reasonable development.

But now Nadine was home, and looking darn good. Jamal subconsciously licked his lips reflecting on their coffee date.

Nadine had always been his best friend, the only person who really knew his heart. He fingered the Matchbox cars that were lined on his mantelpiece. All gifts from Nadine.

Jamal kicked the leg of his coffee table in frustration. He loved Nadine, of that he was sure. But he had led Angelique to believe they were getting married, and it would crush her if he called it off.

Besides, he was a man of God and a man of his word.

His heard a key turning in the lock of his front door, and he knew it was Angelique. His fiancée. The other woman he loved. He pulled himself together; couldn't let her see him twisted.

"Hey Angel," he said as she strode through the living room and tossed her shopping bags on the sofa as if she already lived there.

"Hi, baby." She kissed his cheek softly and plopped down at his dining room table. "I just came from a great sale at Banana Republic and I'm tired."

"Buy anything I'd like?"

Her eyes lit up. "Of course! Would you like me to model it for you?"

"Yes I would, but you're gonna have to ease up on all this shopping before we get married. You're spending up your dowry," Jamal said, only half joking.

"Dowry? You wish. A husband takes care of the wife, not the other way around."

Angelique grabbed her bag and headed toward Jamal's bedroom.

As she walked away, he said in a whisper, "I thought we were going to take care of each other."

Jamal paced again while he was waiting for Angelique to model her new outfit. He could almost guarantee that whatever she'd purchased wasn't on sale, and she probably couldn't afford it on her meager social worker's salary. She hadn't stayed in college long enough to earn her Master's Degree so she was scratching by on less than fifty grand a year.

Jamal compared Angelique and Nadine in his mind. Nadine was caring and sweet, while Angelique was spontaneous and sexy. The things Angelique promised to do to him once they were married was one of the reasons she got a ring. He was going to go to hell lusting after her if he didn't marry her soon.

Angelique emerged from his bedroom wearing a cream-colored, wrap around dress. He closed his eyes and gasped. It was the same dress that Nadine had been wearing at Starbucks.

They had the same taste in dresses – but did they have the same taste in men?

# six

"I don't think this is a good idea," Nadine mumbled as she listened to Carly's plan.

The plan involved the big, scary man that was sitting on her couch. Carly's best friend's baby daddy, Leo. He was going to call Jamal and tell him that Angelique was his woman and that she was basically cheating on them both.

"Don't go getting scary on me now. Didn't you just get finished saying how fine he was looking when you saw him at Starbucks two days ago?"

"Yes, but why can't we just do the engagement party thing?" Nadine whined.

"Because just springing Angelique's crazy family on him won't be enough on its own. It needs to be in addition to all the other stuff we're about to pull off."

Leo cleared his throat. "Listen, I got stuff I could be doing..."

"No, Leo. We're doing this," Carly insisted. "My sister just needs to get her nerve up."

Nadine didn't feel right in her spirit about the story they were about to fabricate, but she finally replied. "Just do it and get it over with."

"My dough, re, mi?" Leo asked with his hand out-stretched toward Nadine.

Nadine counted out two hundred dollars in twenty dollar bills. The price seemed cheap for the amount of havoc he was about to wreak. She wanted to run from the room while he was making the call, but part of her wouldn't believe his report if she didn't hear it with her own ears.

Leo sucked his teeth, chewed on the toothpick in his mouth, and dialed Jamal's number on the disposable cell phone he'd bought especially for the job. He put the call on speaker when Jamal answered the phone.

"Hello?" Jamal asked.

"Two questions. Who are you and why does your number keep showing up in my woman's phone?"

"Come again?"

"You heard me, hard head."

"I think you have the wrong number," Jamal replied.

"Naw, dog. I got the right number. You been calling my Angel baby, two, sometimes three times a day. You better be a bill collector."

"Angel baby? As in Angelique?"

"So you do know her. I'ma have to come see 'bout beatin' yo'..."

"Wait! I do know an Angelique, but I can assure you she's not your Angel baby. The Angelique I know is my fiancée." Jamal answered calmly. He didn't sound scared of Leo, but he did seem concerned.

"Y'all engaged? Ain't this about a mutha? So I guess we gone have to get a paternity test on this here baby."

"*Baby?* Now I know you got it twisted."

Nadine's eyes bucked out of her head and she slammed her hand over her mouth to keep from screaming. No one had mentioned anything about saying Angelique was pregnant! That was going too far. Besides, Nadine couldn't ever see Jamal believing that about Angelique.

Leo continued, "She just showed me two lines on the pee stick this morning. Don't act like you don't know."

Nadine could hear Jamal chuckle into the phone, and then the call was disconnected.

"Are y'all crazy?" Nadine asked.

Carly snatched the phone up from the table to make sure it was off. "Girl, shush until the coast is clear. What if he'd heard you?"

"Well, he didn't. The phone was off."

Leo took the phone from Carly and stood to his feet. "Nice doin' bidness with you ladies."

"Seriously!" Nadine exclaimed. "That wasn't believable at all. He was laughing and he hung up."

Carly said, "You are missing the point."

"Enlighten me."

"He wasn't supposed to believe it," Carly explained.

Nadine scrunched up her nose in exasperated confusion. "What?"

"The story was too ridiculous for him to actually believe, but it was just enough to sow a seed or two of doubt in his mind about Angelique."

Nadine grinned. "I'm sorry I doubted you. You obviously know what you're doing."

"Exactly. So let your sister work."

A nagging sense of doubt tickled Nadine at the very core of her being. Carly was crafty and insidiously vengeful. But would that be enough to win Jamal back?

Something told her to either go for it and tell Jamal what was on her heart, but once those words were uttered, there'd be no taking it back. She felt like she'd die if he spurned her or worse laughed in her face.

It would be a sweet death. Death by chocolate.

## seven

"**B**ible study was good tonight, wasn't it?"
Angelique and Jamal always discussed Bible
study or service on the way home from church.
It was one of the ways they connected, and kept their
minds pure and chaste while they were in the tight
confines of his Hyundai Elantra. It was a small and
affordable car. Nadine had helped him pick it out; even
gone with him on the test drive.

Suddenly, the car felt too small.

Jamal heard Angelique's question, but didn't immediately respond. He'd queued it up in his brain behind all
of the other drama taking precedence. First and foremost,
the prank call he'd received earlier.

He floored the gas a little making the car lurch forward. He couldn't help it. He was an emotional driver.

"Jamal. Are you listening to me?" Angelique asked in
the whiny voice that Jamal used to think was cute, but not
so much anymore.

Jamal drummed his fingers on the steering wheel in an
attempt to calm his nerves. "Yes. Bible study was good,
Angel."

"You seem like you've got something on your mind.
What's going on, baby?"

Right behind the prank call in Jamal's head was his confusion about his feelings for Nadine. Was it real, or was he just reminiscing on the friendship they'd once shared? He was absolutely physically attracted to her, but then, he was also attracted to Angelique. So, that couldn't be the determining factor.

"Nothing's going on Angel. I think I'm just tired."

Angelique prodded. "I know tired when I see it, and this is more than tired. You should get used to sharing your innermost feelings with me. We are getting married."

He'd never had to get used to sharing his feelings with Nadine. Their friendship was organic. In fact, the only thing he'd ever kept from her was the fact that he'd almost fell in love with her. It was probably the single most important thing he should've told her.

"I got a funny phone call this afternoon."

"Like ha, ha, funny?"

Jamal stretched and cracked his neck as they waited at a red light. "No. I mean strange."

"Really? From who?

"Some guy who says you're pregnant by him."

Angelique laughed out loud. "What? Who was it?"

"I don't know, he didn't leave his name."

"Oh well it was probably the wrong number."

Jamal said, "Maybe I should be asking you the guy's name."

"What are you trying to say?" Angelique asked.

"I tell you some guy called me saying that you're carrying his child, and you ask who it was. You don't say it's ridiculous or crazy. You want to know who called. "

"I was just wondering how someone got your phone number," Angelique fussed.

"So was I," Jamal said.

After a long silence, Jamal asked, "Angel...you're not..."

"Do *not* even think about asking me that Jamal."

"How do you even know what I'm going to ask?"

"You think I know the guy who called you?"

"I don't know," Jamal stated defiantly.

"You don't know? Oh, come on Jamal. This is a stupid argument."

"Okay, you're right. It's stupid."

He couldn't wait to get Angelique home. The argument might've been stupid to her, but it was dang sure serious to him. A man calls and says he's bedding his woman and knocked her up? Jamal didn't find this a stupid discussion at all.

Angelique stared Jamal down and continued, "Nadine wants us to head up one final singles ministry outing before we get married."

Jamal perked up a little at the mention of Nadine's name. She'd looked wonderful at Bible study, and he wasn't the only one who'd noticed. Bro. Gerald Montgomery had circled Nadine like a shark to spilled blood.

Jamal was surprised at how much he'd been annoyed at Gerald grinning up in Nadine's face. Maybe it was because before Nadine lost weight, Gerald wouldn't have been caught dead having an extended conversation with her. Why should he enjoy the benefit of her company now, when he'd dismissed her before?

"Did you hear what I said, Jamal?" Angelique asked.

"I zoned out for a minute."

Jamal tried to compose himself. He'd been doing that a lot lately. Zoning out and thinking of Nadine.

"Oh. I said the outing is gonna be a bowling party."

"That's fine. Whatever y'all decide is cool with me."

Angelique laughed and replied, "That's what you're saying now, until I ask you to sell tickets."

"Why is it that I always have to be on the sales team? You and Deenie need to stop with that. I'm not selling tickets. I am a minister. A man of God. It is an affront to my dignity to sell tickets to a bowling party."

Angelique lifted an eyebrow and folded her arms across her chest – her stubborn stance.

"So I'll put you down for ten tickets instead of twenty five?"

"Put me down for ten tickets."

Even though Jamal decided to drop the subject of the prank call, Angelique's response bothered him. He didn't want to think that Angelique might be giving it up to another man. She was his woman.

Then, he thought about Nadine and Gerald. Had they gone to dinner after Bible study? Was she wearing something low cut so that he could see her ample gifts? His hands gripped the steering wheel.

Jamal didn't want to think of Nadine with another man, but Nadine did not belong to him. His head knew this was true, but somehow his heart just wasn't on the same page.

# *eight*

"I've got a surprise for you, Deenie," Carly announced as the two of them ate Nadine's new breakfast specialty – egg white omelets.

"What now?"

In an exaggerated flourish, Carly placed her black leather briefcase on Nadine's dining room table. She lifted her hands up in the air and snapped open both locks at the same time.

Nadine giggled. "What's with the briefcase? Who are you? James Bond or somebody?"

"I'm Cleopatra Jones up in this piece."

"Okay, Cleo."

Carly handed Nadine a stack of papers with lines highlighted in yellow marker. "You're welcome."

"Thank you, I think. Why am I thanking you?"

Carly took a deep breath. "I had to use all my resources on this one. I even promised to braid my home girl's kid's hair for a month to get this."

"It looks like a page full of telephone numbers. Hey! There's my number."

"These are Angelique's cell phone records."

Nadine dropped the papers like they were hot enough to burn her fingers. "Is this illegal?"

"Only if we get caught…"

Carly picked the pages back up and placed them on the table, one sheet next to the other. Nadine squinted at the tiny print, and noticed that her number was only listed twice. "So why are some numbers highlighted and some not?" Nadine asked. "I'm sure there's some method to your madness."

"Well, it is my belief that a single woman with her own cell phone will call whomever she pleases. Whether it's her fiancé…"

"That's Jamal's number right there. He's got a lot of highlights."

"Or," Carly continued, "An ex-boyfriend."

Carly pointed to another number. It was out of state with an area code she didn't recognize. There were quite a few more entries for this number than for Jamal's.

"What? Angelique is calling one of her ex-boyfriends?"

"Perhaps. And you're about to find out."

"What? I'm not going to call these numbers and ask if he's Angelique's ex-boyfriend. Anyway, what if it's a woman?"

Carly shook her head adamantly. "No. You're not. For all we know he could be married. I've already called it a few times pretending to be different people, and a man answered every time."

"So what am I supposed to do?" Nadine asked, still unclear on the plan.

"You're going to call and invite him to Angelique's engagement party."

"What if it's a bill collector? You know how Angelique likes to shop."

Carly bopped Nadine on the head with a decorative pillow. "Girl, these are outgoing calls. Don't nobody call their bill collector that much! Get focused."

"Okay, so what do I say if he asks how I got his number?

"You'll say you just went through Angelique's contact list, because you wanted to make sure all of her friends got invited."

Nadine took a deep breath to try and clear the nagging thoughts from her mind. She wanted Jamal for herself, but she didn't want to destroy anyone's life. There was a tugging at her heart that told her maybe she and Carly were going too far with their plan.

"What if I just tell Jamal how I feel and see what happens? We had a wonderful coffee date, and he was basically drooling over me in that dress. Maybe if I just tell him, he'll break it off with Angelique."

Carly pursed her lips together and rolled her eyes. "Girl, please. He's too *nice* to break off an engagement with Angelique, just because of some unfinished business with you. He's going to do the right thing."

Nadine rubbed both her arms. She felt a chill in the air, and she didn't think it had anything to do with the temperature. Maybe God was trying to tell her something. "I want to do the right thing too, and this doesn't feel right."

"Girl, do you have anything sweet?" Carly asked. "I need some chocolate if I'm gonna have to deal with your indecisive butt all night."

"No, I don't have any chocolate, but seriously, don't you just feel a little bit guilty for doing all this stuff?"

Carly paced furiously around the table. She seemed more angry than Nadine. "No! Did Angelique feel guilty when she went behind your back and took your man? She knew how you felt about Jamal! Don't forget that part."

"Yes, but maybe I should just confront her."

"And then when she shrugs her shoulders and carries on with her wedding plans, what are you going to do? Still be the maid of honor at their wedding?" Carly marched around while holding an invisible bouquet of flowers, just to emphasize her point.

Tears sprang to Nadine's eyes. No matter how she looked at it, Angelique had stolen Jamal. Nadine couldn't even count the times she'd cried to Angelique about loving him. Angelique never had a problem finding a man. She could've married anyone.

But Angelique had chosen the only man Nadine had ever loved.

"No. I'm not going to be the maid of honor at their wedding, because there's not going to be a wedding."

Carly slapped Nadine a high five and threw the invisible bouquet into the air. "That's what I'm talking about."

"Oh, by the way, I did what you said. I got a date for the singles ministry outing."

"Great! Is he hot?"

Nadine giggled. "He's handsome, not as fine as Jamal, but he's definitely good looking. A little too light-skinned for my tastes, but he'll be a good decoy."

"Ooh. I love a high-yellow man. Does he look like Shemar Moore?"

Nadine laughed. "Shemar Moore messed it up for me when he wore those weaved-in cornrows in that Tyler Perry movie."

"Yeah, that wasn't a good look."

"No, it wasn't."

Carly picked up one of the phone bill sheets and handed it to Nadine. "Now that you've gotten over your little crisis of conscience, will you call this number please?"

Nadine snatched the paper and the pre-paid cell phone from Carly. "Okay. I'll do it."

She dialed the number and at first thought that no one would answer. It rang four times before someone picked up.

"Hello?"

"Hi. My name is Nadine and I'm the maid of honor in Angelique Tilley's wedding. I'm planning her surprise engagement party, and you were in her contact list so I thought you might..."

"Angelique Tilley is getting married?"

"Yes. Are you friend or family? I'm making a list."

"I'm her...friend."

"Okay. Well then can I have the correct spelling of your name and address, so that I can send your invitation?"

"Steven Clegley. C-l-e-g-l-e-y, and Steven with a v and not a ph. 18 Masterson Court, Savannah, GA 31404."

"Okay, well you'll be getting your invitation in the mail! Hope to see you there."

"I wouldn't miss it for the world."

Nadine exhaled loudly as she pressed 'END' on the cell phone. She looked over at Carly who had a pillow raised in the air about to bop her with it.

"What are you about to hit me for?"

"Why did you tell that guy your name?" Carly asked in a frantic tone.

"I did?"

"Yes. I should've called. What if he calls Angelique?"

Nadine bit her lip. "I don't think he will. I think you were right about him being her boyfriend or ex-boyfriend. There was something about the tone in his voice."

"But what if he does? It could ruin the whole plan if Angelique finds out before we execute everything."

"She's going to know I had a hand in it all."

"Yes, she'll know. At the engagement party. By then it will be too late for her to do anything."

Nadine shrugged. "Like I said, I don't think he'll call."

"You better hope he doesn't."

Nadine thought that if he did call and ruin the whole thing, it would be the hand of God. As a matter of fact she was putting the entire plan in God's hands. If He wanted her and Jamal to be together, then He would bless her efforts.

He hadn't failed her yet.

# *nine*

J amal scowled as he watched Nadine walk into the
bowling alley with Gerald. The loser didn't even hold
the door for her. She'd pushed it open herself.

As the couple started toward the group, Jamal appreciated Nadine's look. Long, loose curls cascaded over her shoulders. Big gold hoop earrings peeked through the waterfall of hair. She looked so feminine and pretty.

But then she'd always been pretty even when she was plus-sized. He'd always refrained from telling her, because he'd thought she'd take it wrong. He didn't want to ever tell her that she was pretty for a big girl.

He felt a tap on his shoulder. "Like anything you see?"

It was Nadine's sister, Carly. Jamal stood up and gave her a big bear hug.

"Hey Carr! Long time no see. You coming to church anytime soon?"

"Ooh, see, I gotta get right first. I'm still sowing some royal oats if you know what I mean."

"Carly, you can't get right without Jesus."

Carly lifted one hand in the air. "No sir. No sermonizing tonight. I get it enough from my mama, my daddy and my sister. Tonight, I'm just trying to bowl."

"All right then. Get your bowl on. But if you ever need someone to talk to, call me. You know I'm not gonna judge you."

"Yeah, I know that big brother. You're one of the good guys."

Jamal chuckled as Carly sashayed through the bowling alley, pretending to look for the perfect ball. But Jamal knew her well. She was letting every available man in the place know that she was available too.

He turned his attention back to Nadine and Gerald. Nadine was pretending to learn how to bowl from Gerald. This made Jamal laugh out loud. Nadine was a perfect bowler. And now that he thought about it, Gerald knew she was a great bowler, because she led their team to a victory in the single's ministry bowling tournament a couple years ago. Gerald and his freak of the week had been on the losing team.

Jamal strode over to Gerald and Nadine's lane. He cleared his throat and Nadine looked over at him and gave him a heart-stopping smile.

"So, did you forget how to bowl when you went away for a year?" Jamal asked.

Nadine laughed out loud. "How you gonna play me like that, Jamal?"

Gerald asked, "So you're just letting me instruct you for nothing?"

"Not for nothing," Nadine teased. "I got to feel your arms around me. That's something."

Jamal felt anger rise in the pit of his belly. Nadine was *flirting* with this guy! He'd never seen her flirt! He didn't even know that she knew how.

Gerald said, "Looks like your big brother here has something to say."

Jamal tried to compose himself; apparently his rage was showing on his face. He had to escape before he punched Gerald in the stomach. He felt like a jealous boyfriend – not a big brother.

Nadine grinned. "My big brother is just fine with me being out on a date. Isn't that right, Jamal?"

Angelique skipped up and saved Jamal from responding. "Hey Deenie. You look good girl!"

"Thanks," Nadine replied.

"Come on Jamal." Angelique pulled him toward their lane. " It's your turn to bowl!"

Jamal dutifully followed Angelique, but his mind was still on Nadine. He hadn't missed the icy tone that she used to respond to Angelique. There was nothing friendly about it at all, and they were supposedly best friends. He and Nadine had just spoken earlier about the plans for the surprise engagement party, and she'd seemed excited. But now, she was giving Angelique the freeze.

"I think Nadine and Gerald are really hitting it off." Angelique's whisper invaded Jamal's thoughts.

"He's not her type," he replied in a low voice. He didn't want the rest of the single's ministry to hear their conversation.

Angelique laughed. "You don't know her type! She doesn't even have a type, really. As long as he's saved, she'll like him."

Jamal frowned. "So she doesn't get to be selective? She'll just take what she can get as long as he's saved?"

"That's not what I mean! I'm just saying that she's never had a real man, so she doesn't really know what she likes personality-wise."

"I don't think you know Nadine as well as you think you do."

"You know her better than I do?" Angelique asked. "I'm her best friend."

"Then you need to act like it. You and I both know that Gerald is a player. Have you told Nadine about him?"

"Nadine knows about Gerald. Obviously, she doesn't care, because she's here with him tonight. Now are we gonna bowl or stand here whispering about Nadine's love life?"

Jamal stalked over to the lane and grabbed a ball. He fired that ball down the lane so fast that it looked like a missile seeking its target. He got a perfect strike. Some of the pins even flew into the next lane.

"Baby!" Angelique cheered. "You knocked the heck out of those pins."

He shrugged. "It was easy."

He'd just pretended that the pins all had Gerald's face on them.

# *ten*

"So, I was thinking this floral centerpiece would work best. We can make the church's fellowship hall look really spectacular with these orange tulips."

Jamal listened to Nadine prattle on about the plans for the engagement party as she sat across from him in the local Applebee's. He didn't mind, though, because the scenery was spectacular. Nadine was wearing a low cut, fitted v-neck t-shirt and a snug khaki mini-skirt. He'd never seen her in a skirt that short, and couldn't keep his eyes off her legs.

"Jamal?" Nadine asked. "The flowers?"

"Sure. Whatever you say is fine. I don't have a preference."

"Well, we are spending your money so I wanted to make sure you had some input."

A waitress walked up to their table. "Will you be having lunch today?"

Jamal replied, "I'll have the turkey club sandwich with fries, and a coke."

"A cup of chicken and vegetable soup, please, and a water with lemon," Nadine said.

As soon as the waitress was gone, Jamal asked, "Is that all you're having?"

"Yes. I really can't eat a lot Jamal. That cup of soup will probably be too much."

"Wow. You used to be my eating buddy. Remember how we'd have pizza night?"

Nadine groaned. "Yes, I used to eat a whole pepperoni pizza myself."

"Yeah, you could eat me under the table."

"I was a glutton. That's why I was so big, Jamal."

He shrugged. "I didn't think you looked bad at all."

"Really?"

"You looked just fine to me."

Nadine lifted an eyebrow. "Then, tell me something. Why did you never ask me out on a date?"

Jamal swallowed. He didn't think she'd ever go there. Why'd she have to go there?

"You're one of my best friends, Deenie. I didn't want to ruin our friendship."

"Bull. Guys don't think like that, girls do. I see the way you've been looking at me now, Jamal. If you and Angelique weren't engaged, you'd ask me out right now."

Jamal grinned. "You're right. I would."

"But you wouldn't before?"

"Nadine, it's not just the weight. You're acting all sexy now, wearing your hair down, putting on mini-skirts and killing me with some exotic perfume."

"You like my perfume?" Nadine asked.

"I love your perfume."

Jamal stopped. This was getting dangerously close to him playing his fiancée. He wasn't a player like Gerald. If he ever decided to act on the feelings he had for Nadine, he'd break it off with Angelique first.

It was something he'd been considering, since he first saw the new Nadine in the Starbucks. It had started as a quiet tickle of a thought. Not even a whole thought. Just a glimpse of what it would be like to be in a relationship with his best friend.

But then Nadine started with all of the engagement party plans. He should've stopped her, but then he'd have to tell her a reason, and he wasn't quite sure. He was waiting for God to turn the tickle of a thought into a full grown vision.

"So you're saying that you would've asked me out when I was big, if I'd been sexy?" Nadine asked. She was killing him with that flirtatious smile.

"I don't know," Jamal replied cautiously. "Maybe…"

"So it's all about sex to you? I thought you were a little bit less shallow than that, Jamal."

Jamal shook his head. "No! It's not about sex. It's about you putting signals out there that you *want* a man. I always thought you'd decided to be saved and single. If I had known differently…"

"Bull. You never asked me, Jamal."

"Well, I never asked Angelique either and she's always been thin and sexy."

"And white…"

Jamal puffed his cheeks with air and blew it all out. A sign of exasperation. He couldn't believe that Nadine would go *there*. "That was a low blow. You know that I don't see color."

Nadine chuckled. "You sound like every black guy with a white girl on his arm."

"Angelique is your best friend! You don't have a problem with her being white. Don't make this about the swirl."

"You're right. It's not about the swirl. It's about how y'all just waited until I left town and hooked up," Nadine responded.

Jamal sighed. "Angelique pursued me. I mean, you act like guys have all the confidence in the world. We don't want to get turned down either. Maybe, I thought you'd reject me."

"You thought I'd reject *you*?" Nadine doubled over with laughter.

"What is so funny?"

"Jamal, please stop playing. I was in love with you for years. Angelique used to listen to me go on and on about you."

"You were in love with me?"

Nadine stopped laughing, and nodded. "But that was in the past. You're getting married now! Let's finish the plans for this party."

Jamal sat back in his chair and tried to compose himself. Nadine had been in love with him and Angelique knew about it! Angelique had never mentioned anything about Nadine's feelings; not even a hint when they'd all been friends.

But as soon as Nadine was gone, Angelique had pounced.

Maybe his Angelique wasn't so angelic after all.

# *eleven*

Nadine walked around her condo, taking every decorative pillow and throwing them out of her sister's reach. She knew that as soon as she told Carly about her lunch date with Jamal, she was gonna attack her.

Carly stood in the middle of the living room and asked, "What are you doing?"

"I have to tell you something, and I don't want you hitting me with a pillow."

Carly struck her attitude pose. Hands on hips, lips poked out. "What did you do?"

Nadine threw the last pillow into a far corner. "I told him."

"You told who what?"

"I told Jamal that I loved him back in the day."

Carly lunged toward the pillows, but Nadine blocked her path.

"What in the diarrhea-of-the-mouth heck is your problem? Why would you tell him?" Carly asked.

"It just came out. We were talking and he said something crazy like he'd never asked me out because he thought I'd reject him."

Carly gave Nadine a huge smile. "He said that?"

"Yeah, right after he told me how sexy I was."

Carly jumped into the air and squealed. "Yes! It's going to work. He's going to leave that tramp Angelique! I can feel it in my bones."

"I'm glad you feel it, because I don't. I think even after all of our plans, they'll get married. The God in him won't let Jamal break her heart."

"Humph! Was it the God in him that told you how sexy you were? Or was that the *man* in him?"

Nadine slid down her wall and sat on the floor. "Have you thought about it though? What if he doesn't leave her? Then what? I won't have a best friend anymore after this engagement party, and I won't have Jamal."

"You lost your best friend the moment she schemed on your man."

"He wasn't my man, Carly. I wasn't dating him."

Carly sat down next to Nadine and put her arm around Nadine's shoulders. "Let me tell you something, Deenie. As fine and sexy as I am, I can have any man I want. But I would *never* go after someone my best friend was in love with! There are too many men in the world for that."

"I guess that's true."

"Yes it's true. Angelique is not, and probably never was your friend if she could do something like that."

"She *was* my friend. I don't know what happened."

Carly rolled her neck. "She got desperate for a husband. That's what happened."

"We're not even thirty yet. How could she be desperate?"

Carly shrugged. "Whatever her reason, she deliberately hurt you. She knew you were coming back home at some point, and she didn't care how you'd feel about her being a couple with Jamal."

"But you still haven't answered my question. What do I do if this doesn't work out?"

"You find yourself another man. If Jamal stays with Angelique, he doesn't deserve you."

Nadine wrapped her arms around her knees and hugged herself. She'd be devastated if Jamal chose Angelique. But how could he? She was a better friend, and a better person than Angelique. She used to be a better person, before she'd plotted Angelique's demise.

She closed her eyes and sent up a short prayer in hopes that the end would justify her means.

# twelve

Nadine had agreed to accompany Angelique to the bridal shop to pick out bridesmaid gowns. To say that her heart wasn't in it was an understatement. Nadine felt like she wanted to vomit as Angelique rifled through the racks of colorful satin and silk dresses.

"Since you're my only bridesmaid, you get to pick whatever you want!" Angelique said. "What style do you like?"

"I don't really know. I've never been big on formal apparel. The last formal dress I wore was to prom, and my mother picked that one and my date – my second cousin Roderick."

"That was then! Now, you're hot, so you've got to pick something stunning. Usually the bride worries that her bridesmaids will outshine her, but I want you to be just as fabulous as I am."

"Fabulous, huh?"

"Yes, dahling. I want you to snag a husband too, like Gerald. I saw y'all at the bowling alley. Y'all look good together."

*I'd look better with Jamal.*

"You think so? He's a little bit aggressive. Did he take the vow of celibacy with the rest of the singles?"

"Girl, I don't know. What difference does that make? As long as you don't give him any, then he's celibate," Angelique said with a giggle.

*I don't want a man like that. I want Jamal.*

Angelique's eyes got big, as if she'd just thought of a great idea. "Wouldn't it be wonderful if you married Gerald, and the four of us went on vacation together?"

"That would be...interesting."

"Are you kidding me? It would be a blast! It would be just like old times. The three musketeers plus one!"

Nadine couldn't take it anymore. She could not allow Angelique to take one more breath without addressing the topic they'd both been avoiding.

"Speaking of old times, Angel, did you forget how much I loved Jamal? Because I'm still trying to figure out how you two ended up together."

Angelique turned from the dresses with a look of horror on her face. Nadine wanted to laugh. How could she be so shocked about her asking the inevitable question? The question she'd wanted to ask since that brunch at Pascal's.

"I didn't think you really *loved* Jamal. I thought that was just a crush."

Now Nadine wanted to wrap her hands around Angelique's neck and squeeze. Right in between the burgundy bridesmaids' dresses and the red ones. She'd stuff some crushed velvet in her mouth and choke her with chiffon. Silly heifer wanted to act like she didn't know. She knew. She *knew*.

But Nadine did not commit a felony in the store. She composed herself and asked, "A crush? Stop it, Angelique. You know good and well it was more than a crush."

"I didn't think there was anything wrong with accepting Jamal's advances. You two weren't together."

Nadine shook her head. "Liar! If it had happened that way, maybe I'd be okay with it. But Jamal says you pursued him. He didn't make the advances – you did. Please don't lie to me. If you value that pretty face of yours, please don't stand here and lie to me."

"You're threatening me, Nadine? Don't make me laugh. You're too sweet to try anything. What are you gonna do? Beat me down with your Bible?"

"Angelique, just tell the truth. As soon as I left town, you went after Jamal didn't you?"

"Maybe I did make the first move, but he did the rest." Angelique pulled another dress from the rack and held it up, as if the conversation was coming to a close. Nadine was just beginning.

"If there was nothing shady about what you were doing, why did you wait until I left town? Why didn't you do it while I was here if you really thought I only had a crush on Jamal?" Nadine's rapid fire questions left Angelique blinking. She dropped the dress to the floor. It was a burnt orange lacy thing that Nadine wouldn't be caught dead in anyway.

"Because you were always there Nadine! Always in his face. Always crying about how much you loved him even though you knew your fat behind wasn't going to do anything about it. You can't just stake a claim on a man who isn't interested in you."

"How do you know he wasn't interested?"

"You're back and he's still marrying me, right? So maybe it was meant to be. I never wanted to hurt you. I just thought you'd accept this and move on."

"I was just supposed to accept my best friend betraying me? You were supposed to love me too, Angelique."

Angelique dropped her head and looked at her feet. She didn't respond.

"You don't have anything to say do you? I didn't think so."

Nadine picked up a melon colored strapless gown. "I like this one. I should be able to snag a man in this one."

"You still want to be in the wedding?" Angelique asked.

"Of course I do. No matter what, my two best friends are getting married. I just wanted you to know how wrong you were."

Angelique hugged Nadine tightly. Nadine fought the urge to hurl her across the room.

"I'm so sorry, Deenie. Jamal's not the only man in the world. You'll find someone to love."

Angry tears streaked Nadine's face. Angelique deserved every evil plot that Carly could cook up. Nadine just hoped that Angelique remembered her own advice when Jamal left her standing at the altar.

# *thirteen*

Nadine dressed carefully for the engagement party. After this evening, Jamal would leave Angelique, and come running to her arms. She had to make sure she looked the part.

Nadine chose an understated, tan, knee-length dress. Her black pumps and gold hoop earrings were her only accessories. Carly had wanted Nadine to wear red, so she stood out in the crowd, but Nadine was going the demure route. She wanted to look welcoming and nurturing once Jamal was nursing a broken heart.

That thought gave her pause. Even though she could think of no other way to win him back that didn't include deceit, she knew that her actions would hurt him just as badly as they hurt Angelique.

Carly burst into her bedroom as she preened in front of the mirror. "Nadine, you didn't tell me those people were like that when you sent me to the airport to pick them up."

Nadine stifled a giggle. "I told you they were off the chain. And I guarantee Angelique didn't tell Jamal about them."

Nadine had rented a mini-bus limo to pick Angelique's family up from the airport. Most of them had probably never been on a plane until this trip.

"I thought your plan was lame until I met them. Girl, you shoulda been more specific. We didn't need to do anything extra. Prank calls, ex-boyfriends and fake pregnancies all pale in comparison to that level of ghetto."

"I know."

"And you're sure Angelique didn't tell Jamal about them?"

"I'm positive. She tries to pass her foster parents off as her real parents."

Nadine hadn't seen Angelique's family in years, but the one time she had met them, she'd understood why Angelique had kept them a secret.

She'd met them at their annual family reunion in West Virginia. Angelique had gone, and her second cousin, Remus had stolen her car. No one else in the whole crew had an automobile decent enough to get her back to Atlanta, and no one would take her to the airport either. They'd all taken up for Remus, saying that he was in a tough situation, and family didn't press charges against one another.

With nowhere else to turn, Angelique had called Nadine to come and get her. Nadine had driven from Atlanta to West Virginia to pick her up because at the time gas was cheaper than a plane ticket.

What Nadine encountered at that family reunion was something that she thought was only possible in movies.

On the way home from West Virginia, Angelique had made one request.

"Please don't tell anyone about them."

And Nadine had kept her promise until tonight. She'd cashed in her frequent flyer miles and maxed out two credit cards to fly in twenty of Angelique's family members. Mama, step-daddy, cousins, aunties, uncles, siblings and step-siblings. It was a hot-train-wreck-mess waiting to happen.

It was a costly plan, but Jamal was worth it.

Carly sat on the bed and appraised Nadine's outfit. "I still think you shoulda rocked that red dress, but you still look nice."

"Thank you. I just want to fade into the background when the foolishness pops off."

"Does Angelique know about the party or is it still a surprise?"

"If Jamal handles his business, it's still a surprise."

"Girl, Angelique's mama told me she brought an after-five dress for the party."

Nadine burst into laughter. "Does she realize it's in the church social hall?"

"I don't know. But she said she was gonna be the belle of the ball. I'm afraid."

"Well, whatever it is, I'm sure it will be fear inspiring. Did they like the hotel?"

Carly laughed again. "Oh my goodness, I meant to tell you about that first. Girl, they acted like the Comfort Inn was the Four Seasons. Angelique's step-daddy kept talking about the plastic liner for the ice bucket."

Nadine doubled over with giggles. "The plastic liner? That was important?"

"Yeah, girl. He said, 'Now that's what I call luxury.'"

"I almost feel a little bit bad about all this," Nadine admitted truthfully.

"You won't feel bad once you and Jamal are walking down the aisle."

"You're right!" Nadine exclaimed. "You are soooo right!"

That was the thing that would make all of this worthwhile. Even if she'd gone outside of God's will a little bit with this revenge plan, she knew that He'd forgive her. Besides, no one could block God when He got ready to bless somebody, and she was overdue for a blessing. He was going to reward her faithfulness, and excuse this one tiny faux pas.

Soon, her misstep would be a thing of the past, and she'd be with the man she loved.

# fourteen

Jamal sat in Angelique's living room, doing what he always did when they were on their way out somewhere. He was waiting. Angelique just didn't understand the meaning of being on time. It felt like the later they were, the slower she got.

"Angel, come on! We're supposed to be there at seven o'clock."

She fussed from her bathroom. "Keep your pants on. It's only dinner."

"We have reservations."

"They'll still feed us if we're a little late."

The engagement party didn't actually start until seven thirty, but he'd told Angelique seven, because she thought it was tasteless to show up for anything on time. She said it made you seem like you weren't used to anything.

She would know that more than he did, Jamal supposed. She was the one with the upper middle class family. Her father made six figures and as far as he knew, her mother had never worked a day in her life.

Jamal, however, knew a good deal about not being used to anything. He was raised in a single parent household and his mom could barely keep the lights on. If they got invited to dinner, they were on time – early even.

Finally, Angelique emerged from the bathroom. She looked gorgeous. He'd told her to dress nice, but he hadn't expected all this. She had on a peach colored chiffon off-the-shoulder gown and silver peep-toe slides. Her hair was swept up in a French roll but there were curly tendrils cascading down in the front and back.

She looked like a painting. Nadine would be pleased.

"Baby, you look good!"

Angelique said, "I do, don't I?"

"You're so vain..."

"I am. I don't look the least bit pregnant, do I?"

They both burst into laughter. Although he hadn't demanded that she do so, Angelique had gone to the drug store and bought a pregnancy test to prove that the call he'd received was a prank. He was relieved when the test came back negative, but still he wondered who'd play that kind of joke. The prankster hadn't come forward, so it was still a mystery.

"Did you say we were meeting Nadine and Gerald at the restaurant?"

"Yes, but there's a slight change of plans. They had a meeting at the church, and they want us to pick them up from there."

"A meeting on a Saturday night?"

"Yeah, it was something important, I guess. Pastor was going to be there and everything."

"I'm so glad Gerald and Nadine are hooking up. I think they make a great couple, don't you?"

Jamal frowned. "You already know how I feel about that dude, so I don't even know why you asked me that."

"I just think you should be happy for Nadine. She's one of your sisters in Christ."

"She's also one of my best friends."

Angelique shrugged. "All the more reason why you should be happy for her."

Jamal wanted to ask Angelique, so badly, about why she'd never mentioned Nadine's feelings for him. He couldn't shake Nadine's words from his mind. She'd been in love with him!

Was she still in love with him? He didn't even want to think about that. And why would she wait to reveal that until now, when they'd been friends forever and a day.

But if he asked Angelique about it, then he'd have to mention the lunch date with Nadine. And he'd also have to explain how the conversation came up. He decided Angelique didn't need to know that he was lusting after Nadine.

"If Deenie is happy, then I'm happy for her," he said.

"Well, I suppose that's the best I'm going to get out of you this evening. Let's just go."

Jamal followed Angelique out of her house. As she sashayed to his car he thought about how Nadine had planned this entire party for them, even though she'd once wanted him for herself.

He didn't know much about women, but this seemed like too much, even for a saint like Nadine.

But Jamal pressed the nagging doubt out of his mind. Nadine's intentions were pure, just like she was. No man had ever laid hands on her in an intimate way, and Jamal figured he'd be a horrible brother in Christ if he allowed that first man to be a creep like Gerald.

No matter what Angelique said, he was putting a stop to that foolishness.

# fifteen

"They're here!"

The little boy that Nadine had hired to stand at the door and announce that Angelique and Jamal had arrived had done his job. He stood in front of her, hand out, waiting for his fifty cents. Nadine surprised him by giving him a whole dollar and that made him squeal with glee.

Nadine was in a great mood.

This evening couldn't have come out more perfectly. Angelique's mother, Vernell, and her step-father, Booby, waved at her from the head table. Nadine waved back emphatically.

Vernell hadn't lied to Carly. She had definitely worn an after-five dinner gown. She'd neglected to say that it was from 1972 and that even though it was summer time, the dress was burgundy crushed velvet. Her thin, stringy hair was in a pin-curl ponytail on top of her head, and she'd even weaved some burgundy weave hair in between her straight strands. Nadine guessed that no one at the hair store had bothered to tell her that white people didn't use yaki hair.

The most amusing part of Vernell's outfit, wasn't what she had on. It was what she didn't have on. She'd left her dentures in a plastic, McDonald's cup on her dresser at home so she was toothless and unashamed.

Booby's getup was just as hilarious. He had a jheri curl, but had decided to cornrow the front of it. So he had cornrows in the front and a jheri curl shag in the back. And nobody could tell him that he didn't look dapper. From the top of his head to his curled-toe fake alligator dress shoes, he was workin' it.

Angelique was going to have a conniption fit.

After what seemed like an eternity, Jamal walked Angelique into the party. She seemed to be fussing about something, but as soon as the stepped through the door, everyone yelled, *Surprise!*

At first Angelique smiled when she realized the party was for her and Jamal. But as she stepped closer to the tables, she saw her dear mother standing up at the table waving.

"Hey baby!" Vernell shouted. "You ain't tell us you was getting' hitched, but we found out anyways!"

Angelique gave Nadine a look of horror. Right before she fainted.

Jamal looked confused as Angelique slipped out of his grasp and onto the tiled floor of the church fellowship hall.

Nadine said to Carly, "Get the heifer some smelling salts or ice water. I want her to be awake for this."

Jamal tried to tend to Angelique by fanning air over her face, and Angelique's foster mother ran up to her as well. Seemingly unfazed by the ruckus, Vernell took this as an opportunity to make his acquaintance. Booby too.

"She always has been a frail little thing," Vernell said. "Are you my new son-in-law?"

A Slim Chance

"Son-in-law?" Jamal asked after glancing at Angelique's foster mother, Gloria.

Gloria glared at Vernell. "Go sit your tacky self down, Vernell. You did not raise this child. I did."

Vernell lifted her nose high. "Maybe I wasn't able to do right by her by raising her, but she still came from between these legs, right here!"

Vernell stood wide legged and mimed a baby coming out of her body to prove her point.

"I'm Booby. I ain't her real daddy, and I don't really know her too well. I came along after she was gone to live with them Savannah white folk. But I'm her mama's husband. So I guess that makes me your father-in-law. To be that is."

Booby stuck his hand out for Jamal to shake, but Jamal only stared at him.

"What's wrong boy?" Vernell asked. "Don't you got manners?

Angelique stirred and opened her eyes. She took one look at her mother and screamed at the top of her lungs.

"What are you doing here?" Angelique wailed.

Jamal helped Angelique to her feet, and Nadine rushed over with an almost-believable look of concern on her face. On the inside, Nadine giggled at the blank stares of all of Angelique's closest church friends.

"Angel, are you all right?" Nadine asked.

Angelique narrowed her eyes angrily. "You! You did this!"

"What's wrong? You didn't want your mother at your engagement party?"

"I knew you weren't okay with me and Jamal being together, but get over it! He loves *me* and we're getting married."

Nadine's mouth dropped open and she clasped her hands together. "What are you talking about Angel? I'm happy for you! That's why I planned this party for you both!"

Jamal finally opened his mouth. "Is this some kind of joke? Angelique are these really your parents?"

Angelique rolled her eyes. "She didn't raise me Jamal..."

"But you never mentioned..."

Nadine interrupted, "Why don't y'all have that discussion later, Jamal? People are starting to stare, and Angelique's already made a big enough spectacle. We need to get everyone calmed down and seated."

Nadine could barely control her giddiness as she led Vernell and Booby back to their table. Vernell fussed the whole way, and called Angelique an assortment of names that all had the general meaning of 'prostitute' and none of which should be uttered on the church grounds. Since everyone was still staring over in Angelique's direction, Nadine grabbed the microphone she was using to emcee the party.

She said, "Angel really knows how to make an entrance, right?"

Everyone but Angelique, Jamal and Angelique's foster parents burst into laughter. Nadine was pleased that she could help bring the party back on track, because she had some more surprises for Angelique.

Nadine took her seat at the table next to Carly while the youth ministry volunteers served beverages, salad and appetizers.

"Score!" Carly whispered. "Have you seen Jamal's face? He is straight tripping right now."

"Yeah, he had me worried for a second. I didn't know what he was gonna do to Booby."

The gospel soloist that Nadine had hired for the occasion got up and prepared to sing. Carly started to snicker. Nothing funny about a gospel artist – unless it was Lou, one of Angelique's Appalachian cousins.

The skinny stringy-haired blonde girl started her first selection – *Is My Living in Vain* – the xScape version.

"No! Of course not!" she shrieked. "No-no-no-no-no-no-no-no!"

Jamal gave Nadine a signal that seemed to say "cut it short". But Nadine pretended not to understand his sign language. She shrugged and beckoned him over. Not that she had anything to say to him. She'd caught a whiff of his cologne when he'd come into the party and she selfishly wanted to inhale him again.

As Angelique's cousin continued to murder the old gospel classic, Mother Willingham shouted out an encouraging, "Girl, you betta sang that song!"

Jamal slid behind Nadine's seat and bent down to whisper in her ear. "Nadine...make it stop."

"I can't stop her now. That would be rude. She's really trying, Jamal."

"Angelique is having a meltdown," he said.

"Oh, all right. I'll ask her to stop, but you owe me."

Just as Lou started climbing her way to a high note, Nadine got up from her seat and gave her a standing ovation. Others, probably catching on to Nadine's not-so-subtle clue, started clapping as well.

Lou took a deep bow and sashayed off the floor.

"Let the hysterics begin!" Carly said while pointing over at Angelique.

Nadine's stomach turned when she saw the scene unfold. Jamal had rushed back over to Angelique and didn't look angry with her or seem to be in the process of dumping her lying and scheming self. To the contrary, it looked like he was...comforting her!

Inside Nadine panicked. She didn't plan all of this to fail! But Angelique was working her wiles and clearly had Jamal's sympathy.

"Do something!" Carly fussed.

"But what?"

Nadine wrung both her hands, trying to think of a solution that might work. But she watched helplessly as Jamal led Angelique away from her seat. The two of them walked toward Nadine. Angelique seemed confused and almost catatonic and Jamal held her up with both arms.

"Deenie," Jamal said when they reached her, "Angelique wants to go home. I appreciate you for all this, but it just didn't turn out right."

Nadine couldn't find words to respond. She gave Jamal a terse nod, and he started toward the exit, as the dinner was being served to the guests. Food that she'd paid for with her own money, guests that she'd invited with her credit cards.

Carly grabbed Nadine's arm. "Pull yourself together girl. This isn't over. The damage is already done. Don't you see that?"

"But he's comforting her. He loves her."

"Yeah, maybe so, but that doesn't mean that his love is blind."

Carly's words gave Nadine a faint glimmer of hope. Her plan *had* been executed well, even if Jamal was feeling sympathetic toward Angelique right now, later he would reflect on the fact that Angelique had lied to him. Repeatedly.

"Who is that guy?" Carly asked. "I need to refresh my makeup, because he's fine. I don't usually talk to white men, but he could most definitely get it."

Nadine looked where Carly was gazing and at the entrance of the fellowship hall was a fine, George Clooney look-alike. His hair was short and had gray mixed in with the brown, and his suit was clearly a designer one-of-a-kind.

The most noticeable detail of his appearance, however, was the expression of rage on his face.

"Whoever he is, he doesn't look happy," Nadine replied.

The man looked frantically around the room until he laid eyes on Angelique and Jamal who were still making their way toward the door.

"Angelique!" he called in a forceful tone.

At the sound of his voice, Angelique's head snapped up and she immediately recovered from her catatonic stupor. Angelique's entire body began to shake as the man took long strides toward her and Jamal.

"Oh my God...Steven..." she said.

"When were you going to tell me you were getting married? Was it before or after I made plans for the rest of our lives?"

Every head in the fellowship hall turned toward the ruckus. Steven was by no means quiet with his questions. It was as if he wanted everyone to hear the conversation.

Steven waved his arm at Angelique's parents. "Did you all know about this too? Either of you could've had the decency to tell me."

Jamal said, "I don't know who you are, but my fiancée is ill. You need to back up, and leave before I call the police."

"The police? Call them! I'm not crashing this party. I was *invited*."

Jamal stepped to Steven. "We can do this the easy way, or the hard way. Take your pick."

Carly whipped out her telephone and pressed record on her camera videophone. Nadine snatched it away and hissed, "Stop it! This is getting out of control."

"Yeah, girl. This is some talk show type stuff..."

Before Carly could finish her thought, Steven slugged Jamal in the face. Jamal stumbled back a couple of times but didn't fall.

Carly said, "I guess he decided to take the hard way!"

Nadine ignored her sister and ran toward the fray. She had to stop them from hurting one another. Her plan had gone completely south and was in danger of blowing up.

Jamal got his bearings back and landed a body blow to Steven's midsection that knocked the wind out of him. He fell into the wall and slid to the floor. Jamal turned to

Angelique, but she was already in motion. Running to Steven!

Angelique tripped over her own feet and fell down next to Steven. "Are you okay?" she hollered.

Jamal and everyone else in the room looked on in horror as Angelique nursed Steven. He reached up and pulled her to his face and kissed her passionately. She didn't pull away.

"Why Angel? Why?" Steven asked.

"I-I thought you'd never marry me. Your family said I wasn't good enough."

"I don't care what they say. They can disinherit me if they want. I won't lose you to another man, Angel."

Jamal's facial expression conveyed shock, hurt, anger and sadness all at once. He had the look of a broken man. Nadine didn't know if it was from embarrassment and humiliation or from a broken heart.

Angelique, for her part, seemed to have lost her mind. Ignoring all of the stares and whispers and the state of her fiancée, she helped Steven to his feet and linked her arm through his.

Then, before leading Steven to the door, she turned to Jamal. "I'm so sorry, Jamal. I never meant for this to happen."

When Jamal didn't reply, Angelique turned to Nadine who was now standing next to Jamal. "Thank you for inviting Steven, Nadine. I know that you and the devil meant it for my bad, but God wants me with Steven. I know that now."

"God had no hand in this mess. Don't you even think about claiming a victory," Nadine replied.

Angelique cackled. "I hope you're happy with Jamal. You went through a lot to get him, so you enjoy *your* victory."

Steven and Angelique stumbled out of the party, with her foster mother running close behind them.

Jamal asked Nadine, "You're responsible for this?"

"You've got to believe me, Jamal, I had no idea it would turn out this way. I didn't know that Angelique was seeing Steven behind your back. She never even told me about him at all!"

Jamal shook his head, nursed the cut on his lip and walked out of the party as well. Nadine wanted to go after him, but she had no idea what to say to make it all better. There was nothing that she could do or say to repair the damage.

Vernell tapped Nadine on the arm. "Is the DJ still gonna play? I didn't put on my good dress to sit around here gossiping with these church people."

Nadine ignored Vernell and offered up a prayer asking forgiveness. *Lord, please fix this mess I've made, I'm so sorry I didn't trust you to work out the situation. I don't even have words to express the shame I feel right now. But I beg Lord...please help.*

# sixteen

J amal circled his neighborhood twice before he finally
pulled into his driveway. He needed to clear his mind
and talk to God. The night's events had him twisted.

He felt like his entire relationship with Angelique had
been a lie. She had a secret family and a secret man!
There were too many secrets for him to continue in a
relationship with her, even if she did want it. But clearly,
she had made her decision.

Angelique's foster mother had tried to explain. Angelique had met Steven at a function in Savannah, they'd
had a three month long affair. But when Steven told his
parents that he wanted to propose, the rich old-money
family wouldn't accept a foster child from West Virginia
into their ranks. Heart broken, Angelique had decided to
pursue a safer choice. Jamal.

Jamal would've thought it was a touching story, if he
hadn't been the one caught in the middle.

Then, there was Nadine. He couldn't help but feel that
the drama-filled scene has been planned to some extent.
If she knew about Angelique's family, she'd also known
that Angelique had kept them a secret. If she was truly a
friend to him, wouldn't she have warned him about those
people?

And then she invited Angelique's other man too? Was she deliberately trying to embarrass him? Maybe she wanted revenge on him for choosing Angelique.

He got out of his car and slowly walked toward his townhouse door. He'd talked to God all the way home, but felt no peace at all.

Tires screeched in his driveway and he looked up to see Nadine's car. He kept walking. He didn't want to see her right now. She'd been the planner of this night from hell.

"Jamal!"

He paused for a moment; the pain in her voice made him want to go to her, the hurt of the engagement party kept him frozen in place.

"Jamal...please..."

Nadine was sobbing now, and although he wanted to be cold, his heart melted like snow in early spring.

Slowly he turned to face her. "I-I don't understand, Nadine. Did you know Angelique's family was like that?"

She ran to where he was standing. Tears streamed down her face. "Yes, I knew about her family. I did."

"But you knew she hadn't introduced us?"

"I knew she was ashamed of them."

"But why would you spring them on *me* like that? What have I done that was so bad?"

"No! I was only trying to show you Angelique's true colors."

"And Steven?"

Nadine sighed. "That wasn't even my idea, but I can't blame anyone but myself. I had no idea who he was, but his number showed up on Angelique's phone statement so many times. I just invited him on a hunch."

"Looks like your hunch was right."

"And somehow I don't feel good about it."

"Did you do this because of how you used to feel about me?"

Nadine cried, "Used to? Don't you understand that I *still* love you! I wanted you to leave Angelique for me."

Jamal stroked Nadine's cheek and kissed her softly on her lips. "You didn't have to do it that way Nadine."

When Jamal turned to walk away, Nadine shouted behind him. "So, what does this mean for us?"

Jamal pointed one finger to the sky. "Let God decide."

# seventeen

N adine sat on her couch, surrounded by used tissues and candy wrappers. She couldn't eat too many at once, but every couple hours, she devoured two or three mini candy bars. She felt sick as a dog, but she didn't care. She didn't deserve to feel good, or be skinny.

She had hurt the man she loved.

"It's a good thing school's out for the summer, and you don't have to go to work, because you look like Armageddon," Carly remarked.

Nadine ignored her. Even though she'd chosen to go along with Carly's schemes, a part of Nadine blamed her younger sister for everything that had gone down.

"Stop crying, will you! You said he kissed you! You should be somewhere on cloud nine," Carly said.

Nadine rolled her eyes at Carly and turned up the music on her CD player. She played "All I Could Do Was Cry" by Etta James. It was only fitting. Ironic too. If all she'd done was cry, she might still have a chance at winning Jamal's heart.

"Turn that sad mess down!" Carly fussed. "You are driving me crazy with that music."

Nadine placed the remote in the air and turned the music up louder.

Carly scowled. "I'm getting out of here."

She grabbed her purse from under a pile of tissues and stormed to the door. She swung it open and was shocked that a man was standing there, holding a huge bouquet of lilies.

"Nadine! Look!"

An unbelieving smile broke through Nadine's torrential waterfall of tears. "They're from Jamal! I know they are!"

Nadine raced to the door and snatched the flowers from the deliveryman. She inhaled deeply the sweet smell of the fresh buds. Orange, pink, yellow and white – all of her favorite colors.

Quickly she signed and closed the door. She wanted to read the card without a stranger looking on.

"Hurry up and read the thing," Carly said.

The card read,

*Deenie,*

*I spoke to the Lord all night, last night and much was revealed. I have to see you. Meet me at Justin's, tonight at seven.*

*Jamal*

"So are you still in the running or what?"

Nadine smiled. "I knew the Lord would answer my prayer."

Nadine's heart filled with an indescribable joy. She would go to this dinner with Jamal, apologize again and make everything right. Then, she would have the rest of their lives together to make it up to him.

# eighteen

Nadine had dried her tears the best she could, for her meeting with Jamal. Her heart raced with excitement, and her breaths were shallow and uneven. She couldn't wait to see Jamal again and kiss all of the pain out of both their eyes.

"Are you Nadine Robinson?" the hostess asked.

"Yes, I am. I'm meeting someone here."

"He's already seated ma'am. Right this way."

Nadine followed the waitress to the table. On seeing her, Jamal stood to his feet. In his hand he held a single lily.

"For you," Jamal said and placed a soft kiss on Nadine's lips.

Her entire body shivered as he pulled out her chair for her to sit, and she thought she'd explode when his hand grazed her back.

Jamal sat in front of Nadine with a huge smile on his face. "Were you surprised that I asked you to come here tonight?"

Nadine nodded. "I thought you'd be angry with me forever."

"Why would I be angry with you for showing me the truth?"

"I know, right? You would've never known that Angelique was two-timing you if it hadn't been for the party."

"Exactly. And I wouldn't have known that her family members were extras from *Texas Chainsaw Massacre*."

Nadine giggled. "Now, that's funny. I felt the same way when I met them years ago."

"But I didn't come here to talk about Angelique, her family or her man."

Nadine squirmed with excitement. "What *did* you come here to talk about?"

"Patience, Nadine. We'll get to that. First, tell me about your day."

"Actually, I spent the day crying and listening to Etta James songs."

"You did what?"

"I know it sounds pathetic, but I was so sad until I got your flowers."

Jamal gave Nadine a fake pout. "I'm so sorry to hear that. It's a good thing you got the flowers then."

"They turned my day all the way around!"

"Purpose fulfilled."

"Are you...I mean...how are you feeling Jamal? When I left you...I don't know...are you okay?"

Nadine stumbled over her words. It devastated her to know that she had played a part in his pain.

"Actually, I'm great! I woke up this morning and drove over to Angelique's house and broke every window out of her car, and flattened three of her tires."

Nadine stared at him in shock. She didn't respond because the waitress came up to take their order.

"Can I get you something to drink?" she asked. "A glass of wine perhaps?"

"I'll have a glass of Merlot," Jamal said.

"Y-you don't drink..." Nadine replied.

"Oh, come on Deenie. I've had a stressful day. Don't I deserve a glass of wine?"

"I guess..."

Although Jamal's actions seemed strange, his voice and eyes were the same as always. As loving, gentle and caring as they'd always been. He had been through a lot. And if she'd been through the same thing, she probably would've flattened some tires herself.

Jamal smiled at the waitress, "Bring her a glass of Pinot Grigio."

"Wine for me too?" Nadine giggled.

"We're celebrating aren't we?"

Nadine's eyes lit up. "We are?"

Jamal nodded to the waitress indicating that he was done with their drink orders. Then he took both Nadine's hands in his own.

"We're celebrating the will of God in our lives, Deenie."

"I definitely agree with that! Sometimes we take an awkward and twisted path..."

"To get to the destination God has intended," Jamal finished Nadine's sentence.

Nadine exhaled and felt her entire body relax. Jamal did love her, and even though they'd had a messy start, they were going to have a wonderful finish. She could feel it in her spirit.

"Excuse me for a moment, Deenie. I hate to leave you for even a moment, but I need to use the restroom."

"I'll be here when you get back."

While Jamal was gone from the table, Nadine's mind wandered. She daydreamed about their wedding, and the beautiful, fit children that they'd have. The ministry they'd launch together and the dreams they'd fulfill. Angelique would be a distant memory to them soon, and they'd have their own happily ever after.

To God be the glory!

The waitress walked back to the table with a single glass of wine. Hers. She handed Nadine an envelope and a Bible.

"The gentleman wanted me to give this to you."

Nadine smiled. "Thank you."

Nadine opened the envelope, and found a letter. She removed it from the envelope and a plastic card slipped from between the paper. On further examination she saw that the card was a Popeye's Chicken gift card.

"He's so silly," Nadine said out loud.

Her eyes quickly scanned down the page, looking for the words "I love you" or "marry me". Instead she read the following:

*Nadine, when I saw you again that afternoon in Starbucks, God spoke to me. He reminded me of the feelings I'd denied for so long, all because I was afraid you'd reject me. After that day, I struggled with how I would break things off with Angelique and be with the woman I truly loved – you.*

*Then you made it easy for me. You planned a party to humiliate and discredit your best friend, Angelique, so that I would leave her. And it worked. I no longer have any love in my heart for her.*

*But when you plotted your revenge, you became someone else...someone I could never be with. Someone I could never give my heart to fearlessly. Because what if I somehow got on your bad side one day? What would be my punishment?*

*So, Nadine...I leave you with this...*

*A lifetime gift card to Popeye's Chicken – your favorite – because when you lost half of your weight, you seemed to lose half of your mind.*

*And a Bible. Because you and your sister both need Jesus.*

*Goodbye,*

*Jamal*

Nadine dropped the letter from her fingers. The flood of tears began again – the first one beating the letter to the floor beneath her feet.

As the tears trickled down her face they trailed into the corner of her mouth, leaving not the flavor of sweet revenge, but the taste of bitter defeat.

# The Sweet Taste Of Revenge

## by

## Sherri L. Lewis

To Jashmin,

Thanks for your

support sistah friend!

*[signature]*

# *one*

*S* *abrina Rogers, will you marry me?*
I stared down at the huge rock on my finger, reliving those words being whispered into my ear. My ring sparkled in the moonlight shining through the sunroof overhead. Maybe if I kept looking at it, I would actually believe he proposed. We had only been seeing each other for five months. I had been working for Blake Harrison for almost a year, but the romance hadn't been going on long enough for me to expect this.

"We should be able to get those briefs over to you first thing Monday morning. One sec, let me check with my assistant. Yeah, I know. Late Friday night at the office." Blake put his Bluetooth on hold and turned to me. "The briefs for the Connor case. They're ready?"

I nodded. "Of course."

He smiled and winked at me. "That's my girl. I can always count on you." He clicked his Bluetooth back on. "Yeah, Monday morning first thing. Oh, and the Foster deposition..."

I smiled. Yeah, he could always count on me. I was the best executive assistant at West and Brunson Law Firm and now I was going to become the best wife. As soon as I helped him make partner, we would get married and I wouldn't have to work another day in my life.

"Almost home, sweetie." He glanced over at me. "Only about thirty more minutes."

"I'm okay, honey."

He switched hands on the steering wheel and reached over to caress my ring finger. "Yeah, I bet you are."

I lay back on the headrest. Daydreams of living in his penthouse condo on 16th Street kept my mind off the long drive from Reston, Virginia back to Silver Spring, Maryland. It was the first time in a long time that I didn't pout the whole way home. It would only be a matter of months until me and Blake didn't have to drive to the next state just to go out to dinner. At least he was taking me out instead of me having to sneak up the back elevator to his place. All the secrecy still bothered me, but I had decided that it was a small price to pay for the wonderful life I was about to start living.

When we got back to my apartment complex, Blake pulled up next to my car. I knew our goodbye would be quick as always since we couldn't chance being seen in my parking lot together.

He walked around to my side of the car and opened it for me. I took his extended hand and with one sweep, he pulled me into his arms. He planted a soft kiss on my lips. "So do I get to come upstairs tonight?"

I pulled back a little, but not out of his arms. "You know the rule. No nookie until I get the ring."

He held up my left hand. "What do you call this thing on your finger?"

I laughed and pushed him away. "I mean the wedding ring, silly. This is the engagement ring."

He clenched his jaw. "Stop playing games, Sabrina."

I saw a bit of anger flash across his face. I had seen the same look in his eyes when he got really mad at work. For a second, I felt nervous.

"I'm not playing games, Blakey." I put the sweetest, most innocent look on my face and stroked a finger across his cheek. "You know I'm a church girl and you ain't getting none before we say I do."

His jaw loosened only a little.

"Remember that's what you love about me, I'm the good Christian girl that reminds you of your Mama."

The smile came back across his face. "Yes, that is what I love about you." He kissed me on the nose. "I don't think I've ever met a woman as pure and innocent as you, Sabrina Rogers." He gave me that intense admiring look of his that made me know for sure that what everybody said about us was wrong. Blake really did love me.

He handed me a blue ring box. "This is for you to keep the ring in. You wouldn't want to lose it. Much as I paid for it."

I took the box and gave him a confused look.

He let out a heavy sigh. "Come on, Sabrina. You know you can't wear it to work. How would you explain it? No one can know we're engaged yet."

"But –"

"But what? If Brunson's assistant asks you who you're engaged to, what are you going to tell her? The last thing we need is that nosy broad all up in our business."

He was right. Paris could get some juicy information first thing in the morning and by the end of the day, every person in every department of our huge office would know about it.

"I can't have anything affecting this decision. There's no one as qualified as me or who works as hard as me in that whole office. Who else could they even be considering for partner? " Blake tilted my chin up to put one last kiss on my lips. "It'll only be a few more months, honey. And then the whole world will know. Can you be a little more patient with me?"

I gave him a reassuring smile and nodded.

"That's my girl."

I watched him driving away in his S Class Mercedes and looked over at my own car. Pretty soon, I wouldn't be driving a Toyota Corolla anymore. I tried to imagine what kind of car he would buy me. A man like Blake Harrison wouldn't have his wife driving around town in just any old thing.

I glanced at my car again and noticed an envelope on the windshield. My name was typed in large bold print across the front of it. I pulled it out from under the wiper blade, looking over my shoulder, wondering who could have put it there.

I tucked it under my arm and practically floated up the steps into my apartment. What kind of wedding dress would I wear? Where would we get married? We might as well run off and get married because I had no family and Blake wasn't really connected to his. We could have the ceremony and our honeymoon on an exotic island somewhere. That would be exciting. I had barely been out of Maryland before, let alone to another country.

I looked around my apartment. It had served me well, but I was looking forward to getting out of here for good. I'd get rid of all my furniture the day before I said, "I do". None of my Wal Mart, Target, and on a good day, IKEA specials were good enough for 16th Street.

I laid the envelope on my breakfast room table and danced around the kitchen for a few minutes. I was going to be Mrs. Blake Harrison. I'd have a maid to clean my house and wash my clothes. I'd have a cook to prepare our gourmet meals. I wouldn't have to buy no-name brands from the grocery store ever again.

I sashayed back to my bedroom and threw open my closet, wrinkling my nose at my TJ Maxx, Ross, and Marshall's wardrobe. Soon, I'd wear only the finest designer clothes and shoes – and not from an off-rack store either. Maybe I'd even have my clothes specially made for me by my own personal tailor.

I flopped back onto my bed and held my left hand up in the air, admiring my ring. What would we name our children? Blake Jr. of course would be our son. And hopefully he'd let me name our daughter after my grandmother. Although Bessie wasn't very rich sounding. Maybe her middle name could be Bessette or something like that.

I laid there for a few minutes, daydreaming about my glorious future. As my eyes fluttered shut, the sight of the mysterious envelope sitting on my table drifted into my mind. I had forgotten all about it. I couldn't imagine who had left it. Curiosity got the best of me, so I hopped up off the bed and did a little princess dance down the hall to get it. I skipped back down the hall to my bedroom and plopped onto the bed to open it. I sat there with it pressed to my chest for a few minutes trying to imagine what was inside.

Maybe it was a surprise from Blake. Like a trip to the spa or a gift certificate to Macy's or something. Yeah, that was it. He must have had a courier bring it over while we were out to dinner.

I carefully opened the envelope, wanting to preserve it and whatever was inside for my keepsake box. A letter typed in that same bold font on expensive stationary fell out.

It opened with four words that made my heart stop:

HE'S CHEATING ON US!!!

# two

L ast night, I should have had the sweetest sleep of my life filled with dreams of the prosperous new life I was going to live. Instead, I was awake the whole night with the contents of that letter flashing through my mind.

The opening sentence alone was bad enough. Not only did it say that the love of my life was cheating on me. The fact that she said "us" hinted that there was more than one "other woman".

My first thought was to ignore the whole thing. Blake was an amazing man that any woman would want. I was sure that some jealous hoochie who had her sights on him was plotting on how to get rid of me so she could have him for herself.

But as I read the rest of the letter I realized that this woman – whoever she was – knew intimate details about Blake that only someone close to him would have known.

She mentioned a lot of general stuff like his clothing and shoes sizes, his suit preferences and his precious watch collection. Anybody doing a little research could figure that stuff out. Then she mentioned all his favorite foods and exactly how he liked them prepared. Blake was so particular about everything down to the brand of food he had to have. But still, somebody could have gotten that information from his cook.

I think I got worried the most when she mentioned the things that made him mad and the things that made him happy. She wrote about how he did that funny, jagged breathing thing when he was tired and about to fall asleep. And how he liked weird sports like lacrosse and rugby.

According to her, he liked it when she rubbed his head and massaged his neck. Just like he did when I did it. But then again, that could be any man.

She mentioned several other embarrassing things that I didn't even want to think about. The sounds he made during sex, what he liked to do after sex, and how he liked to have sex. I skipped the lines that had specific information about his private parts. Since I had never seen Blake naked or had sex with him, I would have to take her word for it.

Everything she said put just enough doubt in my mind that I had to know the truth. I had no other choice but to follow the directions in the letter and meet her.

I put on my nicest suit, plenty of concealer to cover the bags under my eyes and my Jimmy Choo pumps I had bought myself as a gift from Blake. I needed to look the part of the fiancé of one of the city's high powered lawyers. Not the part of a young girl who had started out as an administrative assistant in his law firm two and a half years ago.

I sat at the table in the restaurant trying to keep from shaking my leg, biting my nails for fifteen minutes before a woman walked up to the table. My heart beat real fast as she sat down across from me.

My mouth fell open. We could pass for sisters. Same smooth brown skin, almond shaped eyes, high cheek bones, narrow nose, and thick full lips. She wore her thick long hair in wavy curls while I kept mine pulled back in a bun at the nape of my neck. She was a little thicker than my size four but in a sexy curvy way. Made me feel all skinny.

The corners of her mouth turned upward. "Yeah. It's almost like looking in a mirror, isn't it? Close your mouth, sweetie. You ain't seen nothing yet."

My attempts at looking classy were no match for this lady. She had on an expensive looking, tailor-fitted, business-blue pantsuit accented with real silver jewelry. She carried a large, leather Coach brief case that matched her Italian leather shoes. The restaurant she had picked for us to meet in was one where I would never order anything more than water. Maybe an appetizer if Blake had slipped me a little extra change. Her level of class, sophistication and elegance made me feel like a little girl fighting way out of my league.

She glanced down at my folded hands on the table. "Nice ring."

I looked down at the rock on my finger and forgot I wasn't supposed to smile. "Yeah, he proposed last night." I held it up to let her know that in spite of her class and beauty, I was the one Blake Harrison had chosen. Whatever claims she was here to make meant nothing next to this ring.

When I looked across the table, she was holding up her left hand. Her third finger sported a ring identical to mine. My mouth dropped open again. For some reason, that made her laugh. She sounded more bitter than amused.

She laid a large, manila envelope on the table in front of me. I started to reach for it, but stopped. I was sure I didn't want to see what was inside. "Who are you and how did you get this information about my Blake?"

"*Your* Blake?" She scoffed. "Aren't you sweet. How old are you anyway? You don't look like you could be a day over 21."

I sat up in my chair. "I'm 25."

"The youngest one yet," she said with a smirk on her lips that made me feel five years old. She slid her sunglasses off her face and I could tell that she had tried to hide the puffiness in her eyes with makeup too. In spite of her elegance and maturity, it seemed like she was as hurt by all this as much as I was.

"We range in age from 25 to 41. Range in size from 2 to 12. We all have the same face, though." She peeked around at my bun. "Same long thick hair. One thing I can say for Blake Harrison. He's consistent."

My mouth went dry and my palms started to sweat. There wasn't a day that went by that I didn't say that same thing about Blake. His middle name was consistent.

"You know, when I first found out about the others, I figured he was just getting his last flings in before the wedding. I figured I'd let him play and get it out of his system. But then when I found out he had bought another engagement ring...I realized there was a real problem."

I stared at her for a second. Let him get it out of his system? She sounded crazy. I couldn't imagine Blake being in a relationship with someone like that. Maybe she was some lunatic stalker trying to get him away from me. "Why should I believe you? How do I know that you're not...just a –"

"You don't have to believe me." She pushed the envelope on the table closer to me. "I came with proof. Open it up. Take a look at the rest of us."

I stared into that face that looked just like mine and then down at the ring on her finger, feeling all my hopes and dreams dissolving into a puddle on the ground. 16th Street suddenly felt far away. I fingered the envelope, but still wasn't ready to open it. "How...how many are there?"

She rolled her eyes and picked the envelope up off the table. "Here, let me show you."

I thought I would choke on the water the waitress had just brought to the table when she pulled out a thick stack of photos. My eyes must have been huge because she looked at me and I could see pity on her face. "You sure you're ready for this?"

I shook my head and looked down at the table. She reached across and put a hand on top of mine. "Is this your first time being in love, honey?"

I nodded and tried to squeeze back the tears starting to fall down my face. I hadn't planned on coming here and crying like a baby in front of my fiancé's mistress. Or should I say, my fiancé's other fiancé.

"I'm Christine, by the way." She passed me a napkin and waited for a second until I pulled myself together. "We don't have to do this. You don't have to see the pictures, I mean. You can just take my word for it and walk away from him."

Yeah, that's exactly what she wanted me to do. Walk away from Blake so she could have him. I shook my head and wiped the last of the tears away from my eyes. No way I was going to disappear that easy. She was going to have to prove that she was more than some tramp trying to steal my man. "No. I want to see."

"Okay then." Christine got up and sat in the chair next to mine.

The first picture she pulled out was her and Blake hugged up together on what looked like the deck of one of those dinner cruise ships. She was all smiles holding her ring up next to her face. "This was the night of our engagement at the Harbor. Three months ago."

Her eyes went soft for a second as she stared at the two of them, looking as happy in that picture as me and Blake must have looked last night. Her face got hard again real quick as she called Blake a name I would never let cross my lips.

I said, "So he takes you to Baltimore. He takes me down to Reston." Blake must have wanted to keep her a secret, just like me.

She frowned. "Takes me to Baltimore? I *live* in Baltimore. You mean he drives you an hour and a half away to take you out to dinner?" She laughed that bitter laugh again. "You poor girl." She gave me such a condescending look, I shrunk down in my seat some.

The next picture was a black and white and had been taken from a distance. It was another woman that looked like us. Her head was thrown back as she laughed at whatever Blake was whispering in her ear. A third picture had another woman that looked like us but she looked a little older and a little thicker. She was smiling real hard with Blake's lips close to her ear. I looked away quickly, my heart pounding in my chest. "Where did you...how did you..."

"Private investigator." She looked into my eyes. "You okay?"

I shook my head slowly.

"First time you been cheated on?"

I nodded.

Christine patted my hand. "Sweetie, I wish I could tell this was going to be the last. All men cheat. It's just their nature. Poor things just can't help themselves." She shook her head, eyeing the pictures. "I've never seen it this bad though."

I looked at her and figured she had to be in her early thirties. The look in her eyes said she had been through a lot. The tone in her voice said this kind of hurt and heartbreak wasn't new to her. "Why? Why would he...why do they?" I asked.

She stared at me like I was from another planet. "Are you serious?"

I nodded and looked away. I didn't believe her that all men cheated. Maybe that was her experience, but they couldn't be *all* bad. Maybe I could figure out from her how to know which ones would cheat and what made them cheat. Even though my heart felt like someone had just driven over it with a truck, I still wanted to get married and have a family one day. It was the only thing I had ever wanted since I didn't have a real family growing up.

"I'm going to give you this for free." She fanned the pictures out. "Why men cheat." She chuckled to herself. After she shuffled a couple of the photos around, she organized them into little stacks. "Sometimes it's because they're bored or feel like they're not getting what they need from the relationship." She arranged the stacks in order on the table. I was shocked to see pictures of Blake with his arms wrapped around me behind his locked office door. I thought we had been discreet. How did someone get pictures of us at work?

Christine continued on, her voice getting angrier as she kept talking. "Some men cheat because they can't find everything they want in one woman. So they get what they need from several women. Looks like Blake has a wide range of interests and tastes he's trying to feed with a bunch of women."

She stopped shuffling the pictures and took a big sip of water. "Ready? Let's take a look at the many faces of Blake Harrison." She pointed to her own picture. "I'm a lawyer, like Blake. Truth be told, I'm actually smarter than Blake. So I fulfill his need for a brilliant woman who can challenge his intellect."

She picked up the first stack of photos, all of Blake and the same woman. Her makeup and clothes were real dramatic looking and even though the pictures were taken secretly, she looked like she was on stage or something. Like the world was watching her. She had to be almost six feet tall because she almost as tall as Blake who was 6'2".

Christine said, "This one lives in New York and is an aspiring singer, model and actress. I guess she fulfills his artistic side."

My eyes bugged out when I looked at the next stack of pictures. The girl had on a tight tank top with her breasts spilling out of it and super tight jeans. She looked like me, Christine, and the New York model lady except for the blonde wig she was wearing. What was really crazy was Blake's outfit. Most days he wore thousand dollar suits. The most casual thing I had never seen him wear was Dockers and a button down shirt. In this picture, he had on an oversized jersey with a baseball cap, Tims, and jeans.

"Who knew Blake had a little thug in him?" Christine chuckled. "This one lives in Philly."

She looked me up and down. "Let me guess. Not only are you his personal assistant who waits on him hand and foot. You're the sweet little church girl who reminds him of his blessed Mama – God rest her soul."

"Executive assistant," I said with not enough fire in my voice. It felt like she had stabbed me in the heart.

The waitress came to take our food order but I knew there was no way I could eat. I was ready to throw up the little bit of water I drank looking at the pictures scattered across the table.

"Well, if it makes you feel any better, you and I were the only ones who graduated to fiancé." Christine said. "The model and the Philly girl seem to be random weekend flings."

I thought of the hotel, limo, and train reservations I had made for those weekend flings that I had thought to be business trips. My stomach turned. What kind of man had his woman make his travel arrangements to go sleep with his other women?

"The only one I can't figure out is the older lady." She pushed the other pictures to the side and fanned out three pictures. "I would say she's filling his mother role, but even though this chick is 41, she doesn't look like anybody's Mama. And judging from the fact that my PI said most of their time together was spent having loud sex, she don't act like nobody's Mama either. They live in the same building. Maybe she was just a convenient piece of tail. Maybe she did all the freaky stuff I refused to do."

My face turned red with embarrassment at her talking about sex so openly. "Well, at least I never had sex with him." For a brief second, I felt a little better. It was my only consolation in this whole mess.

For the first time since the whole conversation started, Christine's mouth dropped open and she looked shocked. "Never had sex with him?"

I shook my head with a sense of pride that I had more dignity in this whole thing than she did.

A broad grin spread across her face. "Then honey, you missed out on the best part of Blake Harrison." She let out a laugh so loud, several other people in the restaurant turned to look at us. When Christine stopped laughing, she placed a hand on my cheek. "You poor, sweet child. Promise me one thing. Next time you'll deal with a man your own age?"

My cheeks went red again. I looked down at the table.

She sat back in her chair and downed the glass of wine the waitress had brought at her request. She slammed the glass down on the table so hard I thought it would break.

"Remember this." She gave me a serious look. "When you wade through all that bull crap and get to the root of the matter...why do men cheat? Because they can."

I pulled the stacks of pictures toward me, wanting to burn each one of them into my brain to give me the strength to do what I needed to do the next time I saw Blake Harrison. The pictures of the older lady were furthest away and I strained to see her.

Christine saw me looking and slid them toward me. "Yeah, take a good look. You can see how fabulous you'll be 16 years from now."

I picked up the pictures, staring into the older, thicker woman's beautiful face. I closed my eyes, shook my head, and stared at them again. I let out a gasping breath.

It couldn't be. I looked at that last picture that gave it away. As seemed to be his habit, Blake was whispering something in her ear. With her head thrown back, mouth wide open, I could almost hear that familiar laugh bellowing out. I hadn't heard it in more than ten years, but it was a sound you could never forget.

I started shaking so hard, I dropped all the pictures. Christine picked them up, shoved them into the envelope and then stared at me with concern in your eyes. "What's wrong, honey? Are you okay?"

I shook my head and could barely get the words out. "That's...that's my mother."

# three

I honestly don't know how I made it back to my apartment. After I recognized that face in those photos, I just got up and took off running. Christine called out after me, but I just kept running until I didn't hear her voice anymore. I didn't remember getting in my car or starting it up or driving the twenty minute drive home.

I sat in my car parked in front of my apartment and finally broke down. I didn't know what tore me up the most. Finding out who Blake Harrison really was or finding out that my so-called fiancé had slept with my...mother.

I screamed out loud and banged both fists on the steering wheel. I thought I hated her as much as you could hate any person before, but I felt new levels of hate rising up in me. My grandmother had always warned me that my hate for my mother would eat me up one day and right now I believed it would. I knew, sure as I was black – as grandma used to say – if I saw her right now, I would kill her.

I kept screaming and banging until my head hurt and my voice was raw. It never occurred to me that someone might hear me or see me. If they did, I was surely gonna get carried off to the crazy house.

Maybe that was where I belonged. Because I was crazy to believe that someone like Blake Harrison could have actually loved me and wanted to marry me. That thought had crossed my mind so many times during our whirlwind romance. Why would someone like him pick someone like me? I had thought it was God's blessing.

I let out another scream. This was no blessing. It was a curse.

There was a soft knock on the passenger's side window. I looked through my swollen eyes to see who it was. Just when I didn't think this situation could get any worse.

It was Gerald Dawson, one of my neighbors. He had taken me out to dinner a few times and to a few movies. We had even gone to church together and out for Sunday brunch afterwards. He was a really sweet guy and I actually had enjoyed our dates, but when Blake first expressed an interest in me, I dropped Gerald like a hot potato. A simple guy like him didn't hold a candle to a man like Blake so I dismissed him without a second thought. I guess this was divine justice, him getting to see me all tore up over Blake a few months after I hurt his feelings.

He knocked again. "Sabrina, you okay?"

I dug in my purse and found some old crumbly tissue and dried my face. I tried to wave him away, but he came around to my side of the car and opened the door. "What's going on? Is everything alright?"

"I'm fine. Please. Just go away."

"You don't look fine. Is there anything I can help you with? Did someone die or something?" He was so dog-gone sweet, just like he had been every time we went out. Made me feel even worse. The tears started flowing again and I dropped my head onto the steering wheel.

"No. Nothing like that."

"Okay." He shifted from side to side for a second. "Is there anyone I can call for you? I hate leaving you alone like this."

"No. Please just go." I made myself smile at him. "I'm fine. Really."

"Okay. Well if you need anything call me. You still have my number?" His eyes were hopeful.

I nodded. I couldn't tell him I had deleted his number from my phone after my third date with Blake. "Thanks, Gerald."

He patted me on the shoulder and left.

Somehow I dragged myself into my apartment. I closed the door and leaned back on it, crying real hard at the thought that there really was no one he could call.

I lost my best friend, Janine, over an argument we had when I confided in her about my relationship with Blake. She had said a bunch of stuff that I thought was mean and jealous then, but I now knew to be the truth. She had apologized and tried to make up, but I had dissed her too, looking forward to the new set of classier friends I would have in Blake Harrison's world.

Janine still called me once a week – every week – and left the sweetest messages about how much she loved me; inviting me to go places and hang out with her. I always ignored her, thinking she'd get the picture, but every week, right on schedule, her name would show up on my caller ID. The rest of our circle of friends didn't take so kindly to being ignored and had stopped calling. There was no way I could call any of them now.

I hadn't been to church in months. I worked so hard for Blake during the week that I needed Sundays off. It was wrong, but I figured I'd have time for God later when I was married, well off and didn't need to work anymore.

I cried all the way down the hall to my bedroom, peeled off my suit and crawled into bed. I prayed for sleep but all sorts of thoughts kept creeping into my mind. Those brown, beautiful faces flashed through my mind, one by one. How had Blake managed to juggle all of us? I guess I was his Friday evening girl. He must have gone to Baltimore on Saturdays and Sundays. He had his occasional weekend trips to Philly and New York. And then my mother...

I screamed so hard I was sure my neighbors would call the police because they thought someone was trying to kill me. I cried until my voice was ragged. When I finally quieted down to occasional sniffles and sobs, my cell phone chimed to let me know a text message had come through. It was from Blake.

*Dinner plans at the club got cancelled so you can come over for a nice dinner with your future husband. Remember to use the service elevator.*

Dinner plans got cancelled? I bet they did. I was sure he had planned to be in Baltimore with Christine. So since she had cancelled, I was supposed to drop every-thing and go have dinner with him? Did he make Chris-tine the lawyer use the service elevator?

I threw the cell phone across the room. It hit the wall with a loud bang and then fell into pieces on the floor. Next thing I knew, I had jumped out of bed, threw on some jeans and a top. After I pulled on my tennis shoes, I ran toward the kitchen and started pulling open drawers.

Blake knew me as the little, innocent church girl. He didn't know that before I got all saved and holy, I was raised by a mother who would cut a man real good without thinking twice. I had seen her stuff a butcher knife in her purse many a time before she'd go running out the door, yelling some guy's name mixed with a bunch of cuss words. She'd come home, calmly wash the knife and put it back in the kitchen drawer. All she would say was, "Sometimes, a woman just has to let a man know..."

It was only after my mother ran off and left me that my grandmother started taking me to church. Grandma said she couldn't have me turning out like my mother – being all wild, getting pregnant, and leaving her with another child to raise.

I shoved a couple of kitchen knives into my purse. I wasn't sure what I was going to slash, but something was going to get cut tonight. Maybe Blake's pretty boy face.

I got in my car and headed for 16th street. I pushed God's voice out of my head. I was going to get Blake Harrison and I was gonna get him good. I had to push my grandmother's voice out of my head too. Because with those knives in my purse and revenge in my heart toward some man, I was becoming something she never wanted me to be.

Just like my mother.

# four

As I pulled up to Blake's building, I saw Christine driving off in a Lexus coupe with a smile on her face. What was she doing here? Had she just confronted Blake? No way I would be smiling after getting up in his face. And there was surely no way he would be smiling when I left.

My first inclination was to proudly march up to the concierge and tell him to unlock the elevator up to the penthouse so I could make a grand entrance. I thought about the knives in my purse, though. I didn't know what damage I would do when I got upstairs and didn't need anyone identifying my picture as the last person seen going to Blake Harrison's condo when the police started their investigation.

I drove around to the service entrance and prepared to go up the back elevator like I always did. The problem was, I usually used the service elevator to ride up to the floor beneath his and then would call from my cell phone for him to come down to get me since you had to have a special key to get up to the penthouse. Unfortunately, my cell phone was laying in pieces on my bedroom floor.

When I thought of the covert shenanigans I had let Blake take me through for the sake of "discretion" as he called it, my blood boiled hotter. I got off at the floor beneath his and started pacing back and forth, trying to figure out how me and my knives were going to get upstairs. I paced up the back hall, and then to the main hall where the front elevator was.

As I tromped by the fancy wallpaper and light fixtures in the hallway, staring down at the fancy carpet, I realized how nice and high class this building was. I would probably never get to live anywhere this nice. I would be stuck in my low class apartment for the rest of my life.

And then it really hit me. I was about to lose everything. Not only had I lost my fiancé, I was about to lose my job. There was no way I could continue to be his executive assistant. I wouldn't be able to work in the same building. There was no way I could be anywhere near that man.

Where would I find a job that paid me the inflated salary that Blake paid me? I'd have to go back to my one bedroom in the same complex I had upgraded from last year when I got the promotion and raise after switching from lowly secretary to Blake's executive assistant.

I stopped cold in the hallway when I realized I had given up everything for him – going back to college, my friends, my church. Now I had nothing.

And now I was going to take everything from him. I would plunge my knife straight through his heart, just like he had plunged a knife through mine. Did he really think he was going to get away with this?

I heard the elevator ding behind me and heard someone get off. I hoped they were going toward the opposite end of the building from where I was pacing. If a witness mentioned seeing me pacing on the floor below Blake's, I could get a life sentence or the death penalty because they could say his death was premeditated.

*Chill out, Sabrina. You're not gonna kill the man. He just needs to be shook up a little. Maybe shed a few drops of blood.*

I waited until I heard the person stick their key in their door, open it, and go inside. When the door closed behind them, I slowly tipped back down the hall. Just as I was about to pass the door, it swung open and the person stepped out, directly into my path.

Her eyes flew open at the same time mine did. I stood staring into her face. She stood there, staring back at mine.

"Sabrina?" she finally said.

I nodded. "Mama…"

# *five*

"**O**r should I say Roxie." I called my mother by her first name as I always had. We stood there staring at each other for what felt like hours. I was paralyzed by shock and anger. She looked surprised and guilty.

I looked down at her hands. One held a manila envelope with her name, Roxanne St. James, typed in a familiar bold font. The other hand held a familiar stack of pictures. The picture of Blake hugging me in his office was on top.

So Christine had left here from meeting with Roxie, rather than confronting Blake.

"Sabrina…I…" Roxie looked down at the photo and up at me with this sad look in her eyes. She reached out a hand to touch my face.

"Don't you dare touch me," I slapped her hand away.

She looked up and down the hall. "Sabrina, I had no idea –"

"Don't you even talk to me!" My voice was growing louder.

"Keep your voice down young lady. Do you want –"

I snapped. I gathered up all the hatred I had for her from the last twelve years and mixed it with the hatred I now had for Blake and lunged at her. She dropped the pictures, grabbed my arm and jerked me inside her condo. She closed the door behind her.

I screamed and lunged at her again. Roxie dodged out of my way and I ended up hitting the door. I felt my wrist slam and pain shot up my arm which made me even madder. I reached into my purse and pulled out the larger of the two knives and lunged at her again.

I found myself on the ground, face down with Roxie's hand gripping my bruised wrist and her knee in the middle of my back. "Have you lost your Got-durned mind?" Her smoky voice uttered the phrase my grandmother used to use on those early mornings when Roxie came sneaking in the house from doing God knows what in the streets all night.

Her words stilled me for a second, then broke me. I let out one last scream. "I hate you I hate you I hate you I hate you..."

I burst into loud sobs laying right there in the middle of her foyer floor. Roxie slowly pulled the knife out of my hand and I lay there face down, crying for what seemed like forever. It was all too much. Finding out the truth about Blake, realizing I was losing everything, then running smack dab into the one person I hated on planet earth with everything in me. It was enough to make me lose my last mind.

I finally sat up and dragged myself over to the door and lay back against it.

Roxie peered at my face. "For years, I've *dreamed* of the day when I would get to see you again." She let out a low chuckle. "I have to say, this isn't quite how I imagined it would be."

I reached into my purse, fishing for the other knife. Maybe just maybe, I would have good enough aim to put it through her eyeball.

She held up the knife. "Looking for this?" She shook her head, a perplexed look on her face. "Did you come over here to kill me?"

I gritted my teeth. "No. I came over here to cut Blake. You were just going to be a bonus. A *big* bonus."

She chuckled again. "Wow. And Christine said you were a sweet little innocent church girl. You certainly had her fooled."

"I was a sweet little innocent church girl until I found out that my fiancé had been sleeping with my long lost mother."

The laughter left her eyes and a pained look appeared in them. "Sabrina honey, I'm so sorry about all this. I didn't know you and Blake ...I never meant to hurt you."

It was my turn to laugh. "Never meant to hurt me? Really? Since when? Since when did you start to care even a little bit about the way I felt?"

She opened her mouth to protest but then bit her lip. She let out a deep breath. "It wasn't that I didn't care. I always cared. It was just that –"

"Save it, Roxie. 'Cause I don't care anymore either."

We sat there in silence for a few minutes, me with my anger and hatred, her with her guilt and regrets.

She finally spoke. "So if you were here to cut him, what were you doing on my floor? How did you even know where I lived? Christine said she didn't give you that information."

"She told me you lived in the building. I didn't know this was your floor. I came up here because I was trying to..." There was no way I was going to let her further humiliate me by letting her know I had no direct access to the penthouse.

She pursed her lips together and I knew she knew. I pushed myself up off the floor and picked up my purse. All the fire I had in me had drained out and now I only wanted to go home and get in my bed. I wanted to sleep until they evicted me out of my apartment. Or maybe I would just sleep until I died.

Roxie held the knives out toward me. "I could get you upstairs. But honestly, a stabbing would be too kind for a man like Blake Harrison. He needs to die a slow painful death."

"How?" I reluctantly took the knives out of her hand and shoved them back into my purse.

She narrowed her eyes and pressed her lips together, thinking. "Yes. That is the question."

She spun on her heels and walked further into her apartment. Intrigued by any thoughts she had on how to make Blake suffer, I followed her.

My mouth gaped open as I entered her living area. It was a beautiful space, elegantly decorated. She had a creamy white leather sofa and loveseat with a thick white area rug covering her polished hardwood floors. She had what looked like expensive art and exotic looking foreign stuff she probably had bought on her travels all over the world.

"Looks like Mr. St. James actually taught you some class, Roxie. You really came up in the world. Where is he by the way? Did you run off and abandon him, too?"

She rubbed her hands together, staring down at the floor. "I guess I deserved that. My husband died five years ago."

I guess I was supposed to say I was sorry but I wasn't. The only person I hated more than Roxie was the man who had stolen her away from me. Who had rejected me as his daughter and forced my mother to choose which one of us she loved more. He had won twelve years ago and I had hated him since.

She stood there looking like she wanted to apologize again. Before she could open her mouth, I spoke. "So, a slow painful death. What's your plan?"

It was the only reason I was still here. I didn't want to go back and hash out things from our past. I didn't want her to apologize and explain and ask forgiveness. I just wanted to make Blake Harrison pay for the way he had hurt me. After that was accomplished, I never planned to see her again.

Roxie pulled a cigarette out of a pack, tapped it, and then stuck it in her mouth. She had never been allowed to smoke at grandma's house and I wondered when she had picked up the habit. She lit it and took a long deep breath, her eyes squinted the whole time like she was in deep thought.

She finally said, "Christine said you're his personal assistant or something?"

"Executive assistant," I hissed.

She waved a wisp of smoke away from her face. "Yes, whatever. So you work closely with him at that prestigious law firm of his? You know the daily ins and outs of his work schedule, colleagues, cases, all that stuff?"

I nodded impatiently. "Yes of course. That's what executive assistants do." Her snide "whatever" had stung a little.

"Good." A broad smile spread across her face. "Very good."

I frowned. "Good? What does that mean?"

"Nothing. Just let me take care of all this, hear? The less you know, the better."

I stood there with a confused look on my face. Roxie disappeared into another room and came back with a legal pad and a pen. She sat down on the couch and motioned for me to sit down next to her. "I need some very specific information. I want you to think hard and give it to me clear, okay?"

I nodded, still not sure of what she had in mind. For the next thirty minutes, she grilled me on details of our workplace, Blake's schedule, different people that worked in the office. I gave her all the information she asked for, including my contact information. It didn't matter that she had my cell number since I would be getting a new phone with a new number when our dealings were done. And my office number wouldn't matter because I wouldn't be working for Blake anymore. After this was all over, she'd have no way of getting in touch with me.

She finally laid the pad and the pen down. "That should just about do it. If I think of anything else, I'll contact you."

"What am I supposed to do now?"

"Nothing. Absolutely nothing. Go home, get some good sleep to get rid of those dreadful bags under your eyes. Go to church tomorrow and repent for almost cutting your fiancé and your poor mother..." She chuckled and I gave her a look that could kill.

"And then go to work Monday morning like this weekend never happened."

"Work? I can't go to work Monday. I don't ever want to see Blake Harrison again."

Roxie smiled and gently laid a hand on my arm. "Oh, but you can and you must. You have to become the world's best actress because he can't suspect anything's wrong between the two of you. You have to work like you've always worked and pretend like you still love him and think he's the most amazing thing that ever lived."

A sad looked crossed into Roxie's eyes as she stared at my face. Last thing I needed was her feeling sorry for me because I got my heart broke. I stood and walked to her door.

"I'll try as hard as I can. It's hard to pretend you love somebody when you really want to stab them in the throat."

Roxie chuckled. "Just give me a couple of weeks. I promise it will be well worth it."

I gave her one last look, trying to figure out whether I should believe her or not. What if she was just another woman trying to get rid of me so she could have Blake to herself? What if this was all a scam she and Christine set up to make me lose the best thing that ever happened to me?

"Sabrina, I know I've never given you any reason to trust me. But trust me on this." The evil twinkle in Roxie's eyes made me shiver. "By the time I'm finished with Blake Harrison, he won't be hurting any mother's pretty little daughter. Ever again."

# six

I spent the rest of the weekend in bed, crying and sleeping. I couldn't bring myself to go to church. Monday morning, I got up and got myself dressed for work like I always did. I couldn't imagine how I could possibly make it through the day without Blake suspecting that I knew what I knew. How was I supposed to act like I still loved him? Follow his orders like I actually respected him? Be peaceful and calm like I hadn't thought of at least a hundred ways to murder him?

I arrived right at 8:00 am, the time I was paid to arrive at work but an hour later than when I usually got there. I had barely put my purse in my file drawer when Blake barged out of his office.

"Where have you been?" He looked down at his watch. "I've been waiting for you."

I pulled out my lunch bag and put it into the small refrigerator behind my desk. "What are you talking about? It's eight o'clock. I'm here." I blinked my eyelashes a few times.

"Sabrina, you knew we needed to go over the Foster deposition first thing this morning and that I also needed the Connor files sent out. And you show up at..."

Blake must have noticed a few heads from neighboring offices turning in our direction. "Sabrina, can I see you in my office please?"

I could tell it took everything in him not to slam the door behind me. "You knew we had things to take care of this morning and you come traipsing in here late like you don't even care. I hope you haven't let Friday night go to your head. You still work for me and I still expect you to do your job." He started shuffling papers around on his desk and muttered under his breath. "I knew I shouldn't have given you that ring until I made partner."

I clenched my teeth real tight and made myself take a couple of deep breaths.

He lowered his voice. "And where were you all weekend? I've been calling and texting you since Saturday evening and you haven't answered at all. Where have you been?"

The anger in his voice sent a chill up my spine. I had seen this side of him when things didn't go his way with a case or when he felt like someone was disrespecting him in the office, but it had never been directed at me.

I looked down at the ground. "I was sick all weekend. Still not feeling well today really."

"So sick that you couldn't answer my phone calls?"

"My phone broke over the weekend. I didn't feel well enough to go out to get a new one." It wasn't like I was lying. My phone did break. And I was sick. So sick of him and his lies.

"You didn't think to call me?"

I frowned. "We never talk on weekends, Blake. You're either traveling or...busy." I had a sour taste in my mouth just thinking about it.

He frowned as if he was trying to figure out if that was true. He finally came over and put his hands on my shoulders. "Well, of course that's going to change. After all, we are engaged, right?"

I bit my lip and nodded. Christine must have broken it off with him for good, so now he figured his weekends would be free. I wanted to rip his head off. I pulled away from him. "Right. I'll go ahead and get those files off and the deposition notes printed. Don't you have a meeting?"

"Do I?"

I walked over to his desk and grabbed the files I knew he would need for the meeting. I placed them in his hands and pushed him toward the door. "Yes, you need to review these files and you have new client who'll be in the conference room in twenty minutes.

He gave me that admiring look that now made my stomach turn. "What would I do without you?"

I adjusted his tie and patted his shoulder. "I don't know, Blakey. I just don't know."

It was true. I didn't know how Blake functioned before I came into his life. I kept his schedule completely organized both personally and professionally. Made sure his dry cleaning was done and delivered. Bought and mailed both his sisters' birthday and Christmas presents. I did the grocery shopping for his cook to make sure she had all his favorite foods. And once a month, I baked his favorite German chocolate cake that according to him, tasted better than his Mama's.

I had made myself completely indispensable as a personal assistant and had presented myself as a perfect candidate for the perfect wife.

Or so I thought.

I walked back out to my desk and slowly sat down. I thought of all those faces in all those pictures. Everything I had done wasn't enough. He was just using me. To make partner and to keep his life in perfect order. How could I have thought that he loved me? I ran to the bathroom before the tears started falling down my face.

I went into the last stall and locked the door behind me so I could think for a minute. Why had he bothered to propose? I was giving him everything he wanted and needed without any promise of anything in return.

Well...almost everything. Had he proposed because I said I wouldn't have sex with him without a ring? I remembered how angry he got when I said he couldn't come upstairs the night of our proposal. So he just bought me a ring so he could have sex with me? Seemed like a high price to pay when he was getting it free from so many other places.

I thought about talk shows I had seen where they talked about how men enjoyed the hunt. They would do whatever it took to get a woman in bed and then afterwards, they had no use for her. And the more a woman held out, the more they wanted her. Was that all I was to Blake? A challenge?

The more I thought about it, the sicker I felt. There was no way I could work the rest of the day. I came out of the bathroom stall and washed and dried my face. When I got back to my desk, I jotted Blake a brief note saying that just as I had explained, I still wasn't feeling well and needed to go home. He would have a fit when he found out. He might as well get used to me not being around making sure his life ran smoothly.

On the way home, I had to resist the urge to call Janine. I missed my best friend so much and really needed to talk to her. But it would be terrible to call her after dropping her for Blake now that it was clear me and Blake wouldn't be together. I thought of all my friends I had dropped for Blake and wondered what it would be like to try to go back with my tail tucked between my legs now that everything they had said about him had proved to be true. There was no way I could do that. I would just have to depend on God to get me through this.

And I'd have to depend on Roxie to get revenge. And boy would she. I thought of the boyfriends that had pissed her off when we were growing up in grandma's house together like sisters rather than mother and daughter. When Solomon wrote that hell had no fury like a woman scorned, he was talking about Roxie. A pot of boiling hot grits was child's play in her book. Her revenge was diabolical. For a minute, I almost felt sorry for Blake.

'Cause he was about to get it.

# *seven*

I t had been over a week and still nothing from Roxie. No phone calls, email, or signs of anything that would make Blake Harrison die a slow painful death. Roxie had done it to me again. Made a bunch of promises that she had no plans of keeping. And I had fallen for it. Again.

The one thing Roxie had done for me was to keep me from doing some crazy and dangerous the day I had those knives in my purse. Maybe that was all God wanted it to be. To keep me from messing up my future. Not that I had much of a future without a man like Blake Harrison in my life.

Over the course of the week, my anger had dulled down to a numb pain. I no longer wanted to cut Blake. It was time to decide what to do next. I had been doing a pretty good job all week of faking like nothing was wrong but it was getting played.

On the one hand, I was tired of pretending that everything was okay between me and him. On the other hand, it would be stupid for me to up and quit when I didn't have a new job to go to. I had started combing the want ads and submitted my resume a couple of places online. If things stayed quiet, I would wait things out here until I found a new job. How long would that be, though? I didn't have a college degree and there were people out there with Master's degrees that couldn't find a job.

My intercom beeped and Blake asked me to step into his office. When I walked in, he gestured for me to close the door. I stood at the door, waiting to see what he wanted.

"Sabrina honey, I seem to have a kink in my shoulder. Can you try to work it out for me?" He turned his chair backwards and pointed to his upper back.

Really? Did he really expect me to give him a massage right now? I imagined myself putting my hands on him, but not on his shoulders. I wanted to squeeze his neck until he stopped breathing. When I didn't come over to his desk, he turned around and looked. "Sabrina? What's wrong?"

"Nothing...I..." I folded my arms. "It's just that Harvin's secretary said something the other day that bothered me. She asked what you and I did behind closed doors all the time." It was a boldface lie and God would have to forgive me. I needed a good excuse for not having to touch Blake ever again.

Blake's eyes grew wide. "What?" He stood up and walked over to me. "What did she say? Who's talking about us?"

"Nobody's talking about us. Melissa just pulled me aside and mentioned it. Promised to keep it to herself."

"Keep it to herself? Keep what to herself? What does she think she knows about us?"

"Nothing, Blakey." I was enjoying seeing him nervous at the thought that someone might find out his little secret and that it could affect his chance of making partner. "I mean, Mr. Harrison." I couldn't help but smile.

"You think this is funny, Sabrina? It's not funny. You have to be more careful."

"I have to be more careful?" I put a hand on my hip. "What do you mean I have to be more careful? You're the one who called me in here for a massage."

"It's the way you look at me and talk to me. Anyone can tell that you have feelings for me. You walk around here like a lovesick puppy. You just have to do a better job of hiding it."

I started to feel last week's anger rise up in me. "Better job of hiding it?"

"Yes, Sabrina." He paced back to his desk and back to me again. "You can not cost me this promotion."

"Cost you this promotion? What's that supposed to mean?"

He walked past me to open the door. "Nothing. Just...go on back to your desk and if I need anything, I'll let you know."

I walked back out to my desk, clenching my teeth.

A few seconds later, my intercom buzzed. I pick up my phone. "Yes, Mr. Harrison?"

"Ms. Rogers. I need you to make some reservations to New York this weekend. I have a client to meet with first thing Saturday morning. Go ahead and make the reservations for Friday night through Sunday afternoon. I'll take the train."

I couldn't speak.

"Sabrina?"

"I'm sorry. Client's name please?" I just wanted to hear him stutter.

"Huh? Client's name? Wha...wha...do you..."

"The name of the client you'll be meeting with this weekend in New York?"

"That's not important," he barked. "Just make the reservation, Ms. Rogers."

I could hear him slam down the phone. I felt like slamming my own but there were too many eyes around. I was sure there was steam coming out of my ears. There was no way I was going to let him make a fool out of me again. I wasn't about to make reservations for him to go see his New York model mistress this weekend.

It was time for me to give him a piece of my mind. I pictured myself walking into his office, cussing him out, and creating a scene so loud that he did actually have to worry that I was going to cost him his promotion.

I suddenly had the urge to stab him again but the only knife I had was the plastic one in my lunch bag.

My intercom buzzed again. "Yes, Mr. Harrison?"

"Could you get me the nicest suite at the Grand Hotel? I need to have an...extra relaxing weekend."

That was it. Forget waiting for a new job. I stood and marched myself right into Blake's office. I slammed the door behind me and put my hands on my hips.

"Sabrina what are you doing? Didn't we just decide that –"

Just as I was about to cuss him within an inch of his life – Roxie style – the door slammed open.

I turned around to see what was going on. Lila Strauss, one of the other attorneys stood there, bright red with such an angry look on her face that I was scared.

"Mr. Harrison, what the hell is this?" She threw a brown box wrapped with a large pink bow onto his desk.

Blake looked from her to me and then down at the box. "What? What is it?"

"It was just delivered with a card from you that read, 'Hope this fulfills all your needs'. Is this some kind of sick joke?"

"I have no idea what you're talking about."

"Take a look."

Blake picked up the box and peered inside. His eyes widened and his mouth fell open. "I didn't do this. I wouldn't do anything like this."

Before he could get the words out, Kara Hopkins, another attorney, stormed in. She slammed the door behind her. "How dare you! I never..." She threw another brown box onto the desk next to the first one. "For all my lonely nights? How dare you!"

All the color drained from Blake's face. "I didn't –"

The door slammed open again. "I have never been so insulted in all my life!" West's executive assistant burst into the office and joined the impromptu party. Margaret Slaughter was an older lady, in her early 50's or so. "Just in case he can't anymore? Mr. Harrison, I hope you have a good explanation for this."

Blake came from behind his desk. "Ladies, I assure you. I didn't send these boxes. Please, give me a little while to get to the bottom of this. You can't possibly think I would have done anything like this." He laid a hand on

Lila and Kara's shoulders. "Please, I'll have an explanation for you before the afternoon is out."

This seemed to calm them down. He walked them out of his office, speaking quietly to avoid a further stir. He turned back toward me and said over his shoulder with pleading eyes. "Ms. Rogers, could you dispose of these for me please?"

I nodded, anxious to see what was in the boxes that had caused such an uproar. I picked up the card on one of the boxes. My mouth fell open when I saw that they had been sent from Izzy's Sex Shoppe.

I peered out Blake's door to see if anyone was watching. I couldn't stop myself from looking into the box. I turned bright red when I saw the contents and dropped the box on the floor.

"Sabrina! I thought I asked you to dispose of those." Blake stormed back into the office.

I grabbed the trash can and swept the two boxes off Blake's desk into it. "Sorry, Mr. Harrison." I leaned over to pick up the other box and threw it into the can.

Oh my God...I covered my mouth with my hand. I couldn't believe she would...

"Sabrina..." Blake was visibly shaken. "I mean Ms. Rogers. Can you please get me the phone number for this...store so I can figure out how this could have possibly happened?"

I leaned over the trash can, pulled one of the cards off the top box, and passed it to Blake.

He narrowed his eyes. "I didn't mean...never mind."

I walked out of his office and closed the door behind me.

Before I could sit down at my desk, Paris came sauntering up with a huge smile on her face. She had that Cheshire grin she always had when she had some juicy gossip she couldn't hold on to.

She held out a thick stack of papers. "Your mail." She stood there.

"Thanks Paris." I sat down at my desk hoping she would go away so I could try to overhear Blake's interaction with the sex shop people.

She didn't move. "Aren't you gonna look at it?"

"Huh?" I frowned.

"Look at Mr. Harrison's mail." She looked like she was about to bust with excitement.

I looked down at the stack of mail I had plopped onto my desk. I tossed aside a couple of interoffice mail envelopes and advertising brochures for upcoming law conferences. And then I saw what Paris was so excited about.

My mouth dropped open. In my hand were two magazines. On the front cover of the first one was a man that was almost completely naked with thick black eyeliner and a half smile on his face. I looked at the name of the magazine – *Out*. I gasped. The other magazine– *Unzipped* – had two half naked men hugging each other on the cover. Each magazine had an address label on the front with Blake's name and the office address. Roxie had subscribed Blake to gay magazines?

I looked up at Paris and back down at the magazines, unable to close my mouth. "Where did you get these?"

"They came in the mail this morning. I wanted to deliver them myself to keep things discreet. I wouldn't want just anybody to see them. You know some people can't hold water." She gave a little wave and a giggle and walked off.

Blake's office door flew open. "They're saying that the order was placed online using my credit card. They had my name, address, and all my credit card information. How could this have happened?"

I was still sitting there with the magazines in my hand with my mouth open.

"Sabrina, are you listening to me?" When I still didn't move, Blake snatched the magazines out of my hand. He frowned as he studied the cover models and title of each one. He turned bright red when his eyes drifted to the address label. "What in the..."

He looked down at the magazines and up at me. "Where did you get these?"

I flinched. "Paris just brought them up from the mail room."

His eyes bugged out. "Paris?"

I nodded, bracing myself for his outburst. To my surprise, he simply turned around, walked back into his office and slammed the door.

I held my head in my hands for a second, unable to believe everything that had just happened. My brand new cell phone chimed to let me know I had gotten a text. I peered down at the screen and almost fell out of my chair when I read:

*Sometimes a woman just has to let a man know. This is only the beginning. Welcome to Roxie's 10 Steps to Revenge.*

# *eight*

The next evening at around eight, my cell phone rang. I saw Blake's number and automatically went through a mental checklist. His dry cleaning was delivered yesterday. I had given him a copy of his updated schedule before I left work. His refrigerator and pantry were well stocked. I wasn't sure why he was calling but I didn't feel like being bothered by him at the moment.

The phone chimed to indicate that he'd left a voice mail. I didn't even care to listen to it. A few seconds later, a different chime came through for a text. I still didn't move from the bed. I had spent most evenings in the bed since I had found out the truth about Blake. The evenings were too long to be depressed and broken-hearted, wondering about a new job and downsizing my apartment. It was easier just to sleep.

The phone rang again and then stopped and then rang again. Whatever it was must be urgent. I was about to continue to ignore it, but then remembered Roxie's 10 steps and thought Blake might be suffering from the next step. Excitement rose up in my heart as I tried to imagine what Roxie had done.

"Hello?"

"Sabrina, why aren't you answering my phone calls? I'm in the middle of an emergency. It shouldn't take this long to get in touch with you."

I couldn't help but smile. "Sorry Blakey, I was in the middle of something. What's wrong?"

"I need you to come right this minute and bring me a credit card. Drive as fast as you can."

"What's wrong, Blake?"

"This is not the time to ask a million questions." His voice went low and tight and I knew he was trying to mask his anger from whoever was with him at the restaurant. "Just get here and bring your credit card."

I closed my eyes and pictured his calendar and realized he was at a potential client dinner with the big wigs of the Peterson Corporation. Oh, this was serious…

"Well, how much is it? I'm not sure I can afford to pay for –"

"Sabrina, obviously I'm going to pay you back." I knew he was doing all he could not to scream at me. "Just get here. Call me when you're in the lobby." He hung up on me.

I laughed to myself and slipped into the suit I'd worn that day and headed for my car.

When I arrived at the restaurant, I called Blake from the lobby. He had that harried, stressed out look on his face he got the few times he had lost a case. He held out his hand for my card.

"Blake, how much is it? I don't know if I have enough money in my account to cover the cost of a dinner here."

He frowned as he pulled the card out of my hand. "How could you not have $400 in your account? Are you that financially irresponsible?"

I bit my lip to keep from mentioning that growing up dirt poor made me the kind of person that always kept a large amount of money in my savings account. I kept the bare minimum in my checking account so that every spare cent could be collecting interest. In that moment, I realized how very little Blake knew about me.

"Financially irresponsible? I'm not the one borrowing my assistant's credit card to pay for a client dinner."

"It's not that I don't have the money, Sabrina." His face contorted into an angry glare. "There's something wrong with my credit cards. Both business and personal. I don't know what the problem is but for now, I need to pay this bill."

"Of course, Blake. I'll be waiting in my car for the card." I turned on my heel and walked out the front door. I kept my smile hidden until I got to my car. I sat there for a few minutes, enjoying the thought of how embarrassed Blake must have been when they ran both his credit cards and bought the bill back to the table still unpaid. I could only imagine what kind of excuses he had come up with to save his reputation.

I sat in my car watching the door, waiting for Blake and his clients to emerge but a large tow truck pulled into the parking lot, obstructing my view. It paused there for a second and finally moved. After a few moments, it maneuvered its way around the parking lot and stopped in front of Blake's car. My eyes flew open when the driver got out and started attaching his rig to the Mercedes. What had Roxie done now?

After a few minutes, Blake emerged from the restaurant with three men in expensive looking suits, talking confidently with his usual hand gestures. I followed his eyes as they traveled to his car and saw it being attached to the tow truck.

He stopped mid-conversation and ran over to the driver. "What on earth are you doing to my car?"

I rolled down my windows so I could hear, although knowing Blake, things would soon get loud enough that I'd be able to hear with the windows closed.

"Your car is being repossessed for non-payment, sir."

"What?" I could hear Blake's voice go up three octaves. "Nonpayment? That's ridiculous!" Blake nervously eyed his potential clients and then turned his attention back to the driver. "There's been some mistake. You must have the wrong car."

The driver pulled out his clipboard and said, "Are you Mr. Blake Harrison of 1487 16th Street, Washington, DC?"

Blake's eyes widened. "I am, but –"

"Then there's no mistake. This is the vehicle I'm supposed to take." The driver dismissed Blake and continued hooking up his rig.

I could tell Blake didn't know whether he should try to clear things with the clients or argue with the tow truck driver. He turned to the men, undoubtedly trying to explain to them that this was a huge mistake. He shook each of their hands and gave them one of his cards. By the time he finished schmoozing and the potential clients left, the tow truck driver had finished hooking his car up and had climbed into the cab.

"Can you please tell me where you got your information? What is the name of your company?"

The driver ignored him and started up his truck.

Blake began to yell. "You have no idea who you're dealing with. I will sue your company and you'll never work again, do you hear me?"

The driver shrugged and slowly pulled out of the parking lot.

Blake stood there for a few minutes, watching his S Class being pulled down the street. I got out of the car in time to hear him curse loudly.

"Oh Blake! I'm so sorry. Can I take you home?" It was hard to be all fake and pretend I cared. It was even harder to realize that he didn't see through my bad acting. Did this man really pay me any attention at all? Had he ever?

He slowly walked over to the car. I decided to pour it on thick. I ran around and opened his car door for him. It would probably kill him to get into my Corolla. I tried to ignore the disgusted look on his face as he surveyed the interior of my car.

"I'm so sorry, Sweetie." I said. "I know that must have been embarrassing. First the credit card and then the car. Is everything okay? Is there something we need to talk about?

"No there's nothing we need to talk about." His voice burst with raw anger.

"Blake, there is absolutely no reason to yell at me. I'm trying to help you, remember?"

"You don't have to remind me. And I don't need your help."

I held out my hand.

"What?" he barked.

"My credit card. I just don't want you to forget to give it to me. Will you have enough money to pay me back?"

His eyes shot daggers at me. "Sabrina, I'm not broke."

We sat in silence for a few minutes with him sulking and me doing everything in my power not to laugh at how pitiful he looked.

I finally reached over and stroked his hair and then moved down to massage his shoulder. It took a while, but he relaxed after a few minutes.

"Sorry for yelling at you. None of this was your fault. It doesn't make any sense. First the credit cards and then my car. It's all so ridiculous."

I continued massaging his shoulder. "It's okay, honey. I'm sure that was upsetting for you.'

"I needed that account. I don't understand what's going on. It's like someone is out to get me. Trying to sabotage me from making partner. I wonder if it's someone in the company." He sat there brooding for a second. "I bet it's Lila Strauss. She probably sent herself and the other two packages to make me look bad. She probably ordered the subscriptions to those…disgusting magazines." He stroked his chin, deep in thought. "You think she's trying to sabotage me so she can make partner? I bet that's it. Well, if she thinks she can get away with this, she's in for a rude awakening."

"She wouldn't do that, Blake. Tamper with your credit cards and personal financial information? That's illegal. She wouldn't go that far."

"Then who else could it be? Who else would do these types of things to me? I'm a good, hard working person that treats everyone honest and fair. Why would anyone want to destroy me?"

"I can't imagine, honey." I said, sweetly. "I just can't imagine."

We rode in silence the rest of the way back to his building. When we got to the front door, he placed his hand on the door handle to get out and then froze. He looked at me and then at the front of his building and then back at me again.

"What's wrong?"

"Nothing. I...can you take me around back, through the garage?"

"What? Why?"

"Sabrina, please. Not a million questions. I've had a horrible day. A horrible week really. Can you take me through the back?"

I leaned past him to look at the front door to see what had made him so jumpy. There stood Roxie chatting with the doorman. It was all I could do not to laugh as Blake nervously turned his entire body in my direction and held a hand up to cover the side of his face. "Sabrina, please. I just want to get inside and rest."

I decided it was time to make him really suffer. I took a deep breath and used a trick Roxie had taught me as a child when were trying to get something over on my grandmother. I burst into tears.

Blake's eyes widened. "What is wrong with you?"

"Why are you so ashamed of me? You asked me to marry you but you're embarrassed to be seen with me."

Blake nervously turned to the front of the building to see what Roxie was doing. She looked like she was having the most interesting conversation with the doorman, like she didn't plan on being finished anytime soon.

"Ashamed of you? What are you..."

"I always have to go up the back elevator. You take me hours away to another city to go out to dinner. You bought me that beautiful ring and I can't even wear it. And now you're embarrassed to be seen getting out of my car in front of your building. How can I marry you and you can't even be seen with me in public?"

I covered my hands with my face and let my shoulders shake dramatically, letting out deep sobbing sounds. "Do you even love me?"

Blake cursed under his breath. "I can't believe this." He put a hand on my shoulder. "Of course I do. That ring should prove it. The very fact that I'm willing to risk my career and everything to be with you should prove it."

I uncovered my face. "You love me? You're not ashamed of me?"

"Of course I'm not ashamed of you." He looked at the front of the building again and back at me. I enjoyed watching him squirm at the dilemma I had created. He couldn't ask me to drive around to the back of the building after my outburst. But he also couldn't get out of the car with Roxie still standing there with the doorman.

He said, "Ok, here's the truth. That woman in the door there...she's this lonely old cougar that's always hounding me. I was nice enough to hold the elevator for her one day and she took it as an invitation to sleep with her. So I avoid her as much as possible. I asked you to take me around back so I wouldn't have to run into her."

Blake put a hand on my face. "See, I'm not ashamed of you at all. You know how I feel about you, Sabrina."

I refused to let him get away with the lie. "This is the perfect way to get rid of her then. If she knows you're with someone, she'll leave you alone."

He raised his eyebrows. "You don't know women like that. They're desperate. It'll only make her chase me harder."

"No it won't. You'll see." I opened my car door to get out. I knew the doorman would come running. He turned from Roxie and spotted Blake in my front seat. He quick-stepped down the walk to get Blake's door. Roxie didn't leave her post at the front of the building, only yards away from us. Blake looked horrified. I walked around to his side of the car after the doorman let him out

"I love you, Blake." I threw my arms around his neck and planted a big kiss on his lips. I thought he would die.

I guess Roxie decided to let him off easy because when the kiss was over, she had disappeared. Blake was visibly relieved. He put his arms around me. "Thanks for coming to get me tonight, honey. I do appreciate you." He looked nervously at the front door of his building. "I know things between us aren't ideal, but soon everything will be different. You'll see."

"I know. Sorry I got so upset. I...love you so much. I just want us to be together and everything be normal." I almost puked having to say that I loved him.

He kissed me on the nose and took one last glance at the front of his building. "I know, dear. They will be." He walked around to my side of the car and opened the door for me to get in. He leaned into the window and kissed me. "Thanks again. I don't know what I'd do without you."

*You'll soon find out.* I gave him a syrupy sweet smile and drove off. As soon as I was out of his sight, I wiped the back of my hand across my lips. A few moments later, my cell phone vibrated. I looked at the screen and saw a text message from Roxie.

> *Did you see his face when he saw me? I thought he would pee in his pants!!! Can't wait to hear what the tears were all about. Drive down the block, wait five minutes then come back and see me. We need to plot out the next steps in our plan.*

# *nine*

I made my usual trip up the service elevator to the tenth floor where Roxie lived. I walked down the long hall quickly, watching to make sure the coast was clear as I approached her condo and knocked. When I did, Roxie pulled me inside quickly and closed the door and leaned against it. A broad grin spread across her face. "Now that was the most fun I've had in a looonng time."

We both laughed and I followed her into her living room. "You have to tell me everything. I trust the packages and the magazines arrived as ordered?"

We both howled with laughter as I explained the scene in the office she had created with her packages from Izzy's.

She wiped her eyes and leaned back against the couch. "And I was right to guess that you'd be the person bringing him home tonight. I knew he'd be too embarrassed to let anyone else know his car got repossessed."

"How in the world did you do that?"

Roxie held up a finger and shook her head. "Ah ah ah. Remember the rule. The less you know, the better. You let your mama handle the bad stuff."

"Did you see him sweating in my front seat when we pulled up? That was so perfect."

Roxie said, "The tow truck driver called when he pulled off so I was able to guess what time to plant myself downstairs. Now what were all those tears about?"

I told her about Blake's wanting to be dropped off in the garage. Her eyes went wide and she burst into laughter. "You really wanted to make him suffer, huh? I'm gonna make him suffer for calling me a desperate, lonely old cougar. He might get twenty steps for that."

We both laughed. Roxie looked me in the eyes and her voice went soft. "How are you doing with all of this? I know it hasn't been easy, still being around him and all. You okay?"

"I'm fine." I looked away from her. I hated seeing the care and concern in her eyes. I didn't want her thinking we were going to have any relationship when this was all over. "So what's next? What information do you need?"

She stared at my face for a second, with that guilty regretful look. "Did you love him, Sabrina?"

I rolled my eyes. "Roxie, I'm here because you said we needed to plan out the next step. If I had known you wanted to have a mother daughter chat, I would have gone on home."

"I just want to make sure you're okay before we go on.

"I said I was fine." The words came out mean and venomous. I didn't care. She deserved it.

She sat there quiet for a few seconds. "Is it a crime for me to ask about your feelings? You were engaged to this man and now we're destroying his life. Before we plot out the next step, I was –"

"Spare me. It's too late for you to be worried about my feelings now. Were you thinking about my feelings when you left me twelve years ago? I mean, now all of a sudden you want to be my mother and care about what I'm going through? Where were you when I got my first period? Had my first kiss? Went to the prom? Was trying to figure out what college I was going to? Where were you when grandma died?"

Roxie's eyes widened. "I was there when she died."

My mouth flew open. "You came to the funeral and sat in the back and left after you viewed her body. You didn't say even a word to me. Just rushed out the back door."

Roxie's head dropped.

"Where were you when I was trying to figure out how I was going to live without her? When I had to drop out of college and get a job because I couldn't afford to stay in school without her support? It's too late to care, Roxie."

She sat there deflated. "So you're gonna hate me forever?"

I let out a deep breath. "Do you want more information about Blake or should I go?"

She rose from the couch and disappeared into one of her bedrooms. A few moments later, she returned with her legal pad.

Without making eye contact, I laid out Blake's schedule for the week in great detail. Normally I would have been proud to know his schedule and plans so well. Now I felt like a stupid idiot, completely lost in a man's life that could care less about me.

"He has a huge presentation next Saturday morning. You throw a monkey wrench in that and he's doomed." I smiled at the thought of what she would dream up and what it would do to Blake.

Roxie laughed. "Hmmm…I guess you got some of your mama's devilment in you, huh?"

The smile left my face. "No. I'm not anything like you."

She smirked. "Really? You're more like me than you want to believe. More than you want to be."

"How so? You don't know anything about me so how can you say that? I'm not like you at all."

"No?" She leaned in close to me and stared me straight in the eye. "Then why were you going to marry Blake?"

I pulled back from her. "What?"

"Why were you going to marry Blake Harrison? I asked you before, did you love him? Or was he just a way up in the world?"

I opened my mouth to protest and then stopped. Was I marrying Blake because of his money? His social status?

"You judge me for marrying Mr. St. James for money, but yet you were planning to do the very same thing. You don't love that man, Sabrina. How could you? He's as mean as a snake and only cares about himself. But he could rescue you from struggling and living the poor life. You could move into the penthouse, get a new wardrobe, a new car, everything you ever dreamed of. Isn't that how it works?"

I just stared at her.

"See, Sabrina. You are just like me."

I wanted to scratch her eyeballs out. "There's a big difference. I didn't leave a little girl behind like you did."

"Didn't you though? Look at you. You don't have any friends, no life, everything centers around Blake. You did leave a little girl behind. You."

Her words slammed into my chest.

Her cell phone let out a short jazzy tune. She rose to pick it up from the end table and smirked when she looked at the screen. "Just as I thought. After the little show you put on downstairs, Mr. Harrison knows he's got some serious making up to do. I need to get upstairs."

I rose and walked slowly to the door, still reeling from the words she had said to me.

Roxie followed me to the door. "Sabrina, there's nothing I can do to make up for what I did. I would give anything to go back and change that decision. If I had it to do all over again, I would have stayed poor and broke just to see my little girl grow up. And maybe if I had been there, you wouldn't be making the same wrong decisions and choices I made. All I want is for you to forgive me and give me a chance to be in your life again."

I reached out for the doorknob. "If you need any more information on Blake, send me a text or an email. Hopefully, you have all you need to finish your ten steps."

I opened the door. "Goodbye Roxie."

As I closed the door behind me, I tried not to see the tears trickling down both cheeks.

# ten

The next morning I woke up and arranged a car service for Blake to get to work. I knew there was no way he would want me driving him to work in my car. Roxie made the necessary calls to get his car released and I arranged to have it towed to the office so Blake could drive himself home. Roxie did whatever she had to do to fix Blake's credit card situation and all was well in his world again. At least until Roxie unleashed the next step in her plan.

Blake spent the entire morning thanking me and then slipped me some money to take the rest of the day off to go to the spa. I decided to pocket the money and go home and rest. I needed to save as much as I could.

As I was driving home, my phone rang. I thought it was Blake, realizing he needed me and calling to get me to come back to the office. When I looked down at the caller ID, Janine's number was flashing on the screen. It was her weekly call.

I paused for a second and decided to answer it. "Hello?"

"Sabrina, I can't believe you answered the phone. How are you? It's Janine."

"I know who this is, silly. I'm...fine. Ummm, how are you?" I got out of the car and started up the walk to my apartment.

"I'm fine. Wow, I can't believe I'm actually talking to you. Thanks for answering. It must be God. The past couple of weeks you've been on my mind a lot. I've been praying for you. Everything okay?"

I stared at the phone, not knowing what to say. "Sure. Everything's fine."

Janine laughed. "I know we haven't talked in months but I still know you. You're not fine. What's going on?"

My silence for the next few seconds messed up any chance I had of convincing Janine that I was okay. She was one of those people that could see straight through you, so lying wouldn't do me any good. I decided to give it a try because telling the truth about my messy life was too embarrassing. "Work is stressful right now. That's all. Blake is up for partner and we're both working really hard. I had to take the afternoon off to recover."

"So things are still good between the two of you?"

I couldn't dance around a direct question like that. As I sat there trying to think of a lie to tell her, she said, "I made your favorite – chicken and dumplings – almost as good as your grandmother's. You remember where I live?"

"Janine, I –"

"I'm not taking no for an answer, Sabrina. I won't have any peace until I know what's wrong with you. Don't you think God put you on my heart for a reason?"

"I really appreciate you and God being concerned about me but I really need some rest."

"Okay, I'll be over there then. See you in about thirty minutes. You still live in the same place, right?

"Janine..."

"Come on, Brina. Don't you want to see your best friend?"

I almost started crying when she said those words. "You still consider me your best friend?"

"Always girl. And I'm about to perform one of the most important best friend duties. Being there when things go wrong with your man. Should I bring Gummy bears?"

A few tears did stream down my face when she said that. "Yeah. Gummy bears. And Skittles, too."

Janine laughed. "Wow, that bad?"

I started crying full force into the phone.

"Oh, Brina. I'm sorry. Be there in a few."


Janine just sat there with her mouth open when I told her about Blake's proposal and then my meeting with Christine. When I got to the part about Roxie, she fell off the couch in her classic dramatic Janine fashion. When I told her that I had gone to Blake's building with knives in my purse and ran into Roxie instead, she rolled on the floor clutching her chest.

"Oh my God!" She stopped rolling and sat up and looked at me. "You saw her? You actually saw your mother? What did you say when you saw her? Does she look the same? Were you glad to see her? Oh my goodness, Brina, this is really big! God is so good! I can't believe He brought your mother back into your life."

I frowned at her. "God is so good? How you figure? I just lost my fiancée and found out that my long lost mother was one of four women who were sleeping with him. Now years after abandoning me when I needed her the most, she wants to be all up in my life again. What's good about that?"

Janine popped up off the floor and onto the couch next to me. She grabbed both of my hands. "I can't believe you. This is God and it's all good." She jumped up off the couch and started pacing the living room. "What do I always tell you? It's just a matter of perspective." She put her hands on her hips. "Have you talked to God about all this?"

I frowned and looked down at my feet.

"That's what I thought." She paced the floor again, frowning like she was thinking real hard.

Janine struggled to fill a size 2 and always complained about not being able to gain weight. I told her it was because she was a constant ball of motion. She couldn't sit on the couch and have a normal conversation like a normal person. She was up and down, pacing, no matter what we were talking about. Even if we were in a setting where she was forced to sit still, her arms were in motion and her mouth going a mile a minute.

"Janine, you're making me dizzy and tired. Sit down."

"Sorry." She plopped down onto the couch next to me. I knew it wouldn't last for long but at least I'd get a second to rest my nerves before she started moving again.

"All I'm saying is that you need to see this for the blessing that it is. God protected you from marrying

Blake..." Janine rolled her eyes "...which would have been a disaster. And He brought your mother back. After all these years, you get to have a relationship with her."

I started to protest but that would have been a slap in the face to Janine. Her own mother had died when she was two, so the thought of having a mother and not wanting to be close to her was unimaginable to Janine.

"You have to see this as a blessing. Otherwise you're going to miss it. A chance to have a Mommy."

I knew there was no way I could explain to her how much I hated Roxie and how I never planned to let her be a part of my life.

"So tell me about her. What's she like?"

Janine looked so excited, it was hard not to tell her something about Roxie. "She looks like me. Add about twenty years and thirty pounds and you got Roxie."

She raised her eyebrows. "How come you call you mother by her first name?"

I let out a deep breath. I had never gone in depth with Janine about what had happened with Roxie leaving me. She so romanticized her thoughts and memories about her mother that it seemed rude. Maybe I needed to tell her now. Otherwise, knowing Janine, she would drive me crazy wanting me and Roxie to have the perfect mother-daughter relationship. Maybe if she realized that Roxie wasn't mother material, she wouldn't force the issue.

"Roxie had me when she was 16. As I got older and she had her boyfriends around, she never wanted me to call her Mama because she was afraid I'd scare the men off. She let most of them believe I was her little sister."

Janine frowned.

"Yeah. She's a real piece of work." I told Janine the rest of the story – how Roxie left me for Mr. St. James and never sent any money even though she had plenty and knew me and grandma were struggling. How she traveled the world and only bothered to send us a post card from all the different places she got to see. How she walked away and never looked back. I figured Janine would agree with me that I was better off without her in my life.

"But she's different now, right? She wants to be in your life? She asked your forgiveness?"

I rolled my eyes and Janine jumped up and started pacing again. "You have to forgive her. Christians have to forgive."

Had it been that long since I had been to church? Why was Janine's mentioning God every other word and being all preachy getting on my last nerve? Had I backslidden that much in my five months of being gone?

"God forgave you and you have to forgive her."

Janine was one of those big hearted people that was always talking about love and forgiveness. She did stuff like feed the homeless and also served in the prison ministry through our church. Even though her mother died when she was young, her father was well off and Janine still grew up with this perfect life, never wanting for anything. So it was easy for her to be all loving and forgiving all the time.

"Spare me the sermon, Janine. You have no idea what it's like to –"

"To what? Lose your mother and get her back? You're right. I have no idea."

I let out a deep breath and lay back on the couch with my eyes closed. There was no way I would be able to get her to see. I should have never let her come over.

"I do know what it's like to be abandoned by someone you love for a man." Janine marched over to her huge purse and dug out the Skittles and Gummy Bears and dropped them in my lap. "And I love you and forgive you."

She plopped down on the couch next to me. Once again, I had to admit to myself that I was turning out to be more like Roxie than I wanted to be. How was it that I hated her so much and hated what she did to me, but I was making the same mistakes with my life?

"So now what?" Janine ripped open the bag of Skittles and popped a few in her mouth. There was no way I was going to tell her about teaming up with Roxie to get revenge on Blake. She'd never stop pacing and preaching.

I shrugged. "I don't know." I opened the Gummy Bears and pulled a red one apart. "I promise I'll pray about it, okay?"

Janine glared at me. "You're just saying that to get me off your back."

We both laughed.

"And what about Blake? What did he say when you confronted him?"

I closed my eyes and rubbed my temples. "I didn't confront him yet. I'm waiting until I find a new job."

She popped up off the couch and practically sprinted to the front door and back. "What?" She grabbed her head and shook it. "You haven't said anything? You find out that your fiancée is sleeping with four other women including your mother and you act like nothing happened? Are you crazy? How can you even do that?"

"It's complicated."

"You mean you can forgive a cheating lying man, but you can't forgive your own mother? How is that possible?"

"I haven't forgiven him either. I..." How could I explain without explaining?

"What are you not telling me, Sabrina? What's really going on?"

I closed my eyes and put my head in my hands.

Janine sat down on the couch next to me. "What is it? Just tell me. It can't be that bad."

I sat there without saying anything.

She narrowed her eyes and put her hands on her hips. "Are you going to tell me or do I have to use my torture techniques?"

I reluctantly told her about Roxie's revenge. By the time I finished, Janine was laid out on the floor with her hand dramatically draped across her forehead, moaning.

"Are you crazy? I know Blake was wrong but don't you think that's a little extreme?"

"All that is Roxie's doing. I haven't done a thing."

"You have! You've given her all the information she needs to destroy his life. How can you do this?"

"A minute ago you were asking me how I could forgive him, now you're fussing at me for not forgiving him?"

"There's a difference between confronting the man and secretly plotting to ruin his life. This is bad, Sabrina. Really bad. You need to talk to God about this."

"Janine, I don't need you to preach to me. Just be my friend."

"I can't be your friend without telling you the truth. This is wrong and you need to stop."

I rose from the couch. "Thanks for being such a great friend. I promise I'll pray about it. Like I said when you called, I'm really tired. I appreciate you coming over. I promise we'll hang out again soon, okay?"

Janine followed me to the door. "Putting me out, huh? Okay. Don't think I'm gonna let you disappear like you did before. I see what happens when I leave you on your own for too long."

I laughed.

"Maybe I'll see you at church on Sunday? If God doesn't strike you down before then?"

I laughed again and allowed Janine to pull me into one of her fierce hugs. "Love you, Brina. Don't forget to talk to God so He can set you straight." She paused for a second. "Better yet, I'm gonna talk to God. And you know what that means."

I nodded and let her out the door. It meant that something was going to happen, soon. I guessed since Janine's heart was so perfect, God listened to her prayers more. Any time she prayed about anything, she always got what she asked for.

Well, Janine would have to pray. I wasn't ready to talk to God yet. If I listened to Him for very long, He might talk some sense into me and tell me to forgive Roxie like she asked and let her into my life again. He would surely tell me to forgive Blake and that vengeance was His. And I wasn't trying to hear that.

The truth was, I couldn't wait to see Roxie's next steps.

## eleven

On Sunday morning I turned over in bed and actually thought about going to church. Then I thought about me and Janine's conversation yesterday and remembered I wasn't trying to hear what God might have to say, so I needed to stay away from His voice right now.

My cell phone chimed that a text message had come through. I picked it up and recognized Roxie's number.

*Meet me at Meriwether Baptist Church for morning service. Come in late and sit in the balcony. Don't allow yourself to be seen.*

Oh boy. That was Blake's church that I had never been allowed to attend with him. What did Roxie have up her sleeve now?

I followed her instructions and snuck up to the balcony at 10:25 for the 10am service. I sat on an end row in the back. A few minutes later, I saw Roxie slip in at the opposite end of the balcony. She slid into a seat and took off her large sunglasses. She looked around until she saw me. She winked and gave me small smile. I nodded and returned a small smile. Then I sat back in my seat and waited for the show to begin.

Thankfully I had gotten there late to miss most of the boring service. Blake went to a sadity, upper crusty church with absolutely no spirit whatsoever. All the rich important people in DC went there, more to show off their fancy cars and clothes rather than to praise God. It was so stiff in there, you better not clap your hands other than a polite pitty-pat after a song. And don't even think about saying "Hallelujah" or "praise the Lord" out loud. Everyone would turn around and give you a look that let you know not to disrupt their service like that.

I sat through most of the boring sermon wondering what possible message anyone could have gotten out of it. The pastor had been talking for twenty minutes and I didn't see, hear, or feel Jesus in anything he said.

It seemed like his sermon was timed to end after exactly twenty-five minutes. The deacons stood across the front to give an altar call. I looked over at Roxie to see if I had missed something. Church was about to end and nothing had happened. She saw the question in my eyes and winked again and then smiled such an evil smile that I was afraid for Blake as to what was about to happen next.

A nice looking family went up to the altar to join the church. And then I heard a loud wailing. The church went silent except for the organ playing "Come To Jesus". The wailing got louder as a woman with a blonde weave approached the altar. She fell to her knees when she reached the front. One of the deacons reached to pat her on the back, and it seemed to make the wailing louder. He looked around for help and one of the church mothers came with a fan, as if flapping it wildly would calm whatever was wrong with this woman.

The pastor didn't seem to know what to do with such an emotional outburst in his church and kept his distance in the pulpit. The deacons looked to him to come restore the decorum to their stodgy service. The woman finally stood to her feet. "Thank you Jesus, Thank You Jesus."

She wore a red hot dress that fit all her curves in all the right places and looked more appropriate for the club on Saturday night rather than church on Sunday morning. I looked closer and realized why she looked familiar.

She had our face. It was the Philly girl. Oh dear. What had Roxie done?

"Thank you Jesus." She rocked and moaned. The deacon patted her shoulder, seeming relieved that she had chosen to calm down some. The pastor came down from the pulpit to the family that approached the altar and spoke quietly to them. He then turned to the congregation and said, "Meriwether Baptist Church, we have the Hunt family joining us on their Christian experience. Please give them a hand to welcome them."

He walked over to the Philly girl and spoke quietly to her. She had calmed herself down enough to have a conversation with him. Next thing you know, she pulled the microphone out of his hand and said, "I just need to thank Jesus and share my testimony." The pastor looked shocked. When he went to take the mic out of her hand, she stepped away a little and continued to address the crowd. "Saints, please pray for me. I found out some terrible news this week. I went to the doctor and found out that I was HIV positive."

A ripple of murmurs scattered across the congregation. The pastor looked too shocked to move.

Philly girl kept on talking. "I came here to confront the person who gave it to me. I really came to kill him. But during the service, the Lord touched my heart and I've been able to forgive." She lifted her arms in the air. "Blake Harrison, I forgive you for ruining my life. I forgive you for giving me this horrible disease. I came here to kill you but God has spared you. So now I forgive you. I forgive you." There was a loud stir in the congregation as the pastor finally succeeded in wrestling the microphone out of her hand.

She threw her hands in the air again and began moaning and rocking, "Thank you Jesus. Thank you Jesus."

I stared over at Roxie with my mouth open. She put her finger on her chin and gestured upward. I closed my mouth. I started to get up and leave but she held up a finger and shook her head slightly. I sat back down and followed her eyes to the lower level. A few minutes later, I saw Blake rise from the third pew, his long strides quickly taking him out of view.

A few minutes later, my phone vibrated. I looked down at the text on the screen. It was from Blake.

*Cancel all my appointments for tomorrow. I need to go to the doctor.*

Minutes later, Roxie put on her sunglasses, held up five fingers and exited down the back steps.

I sat there, unable to believe what had just happened. I counted in my head. Sex toys, gay magazines, credit cards, car repossessed. If this was only step five of ten in her revenge plan, I was scared for Blake at the thought of what might happen next.

# twelve

I sat in the balcony until I was sure both Blake and Roxie were gone. I hadn't felt God one bit during that dry boring service, but I was sure feeling Him right now. The conviction was about to eat me up. Blake had done us all wrong – especially me and Christine – but he didn't deserve what we had just done. If Roxie kept it up, he could lose everything. His job and his reputation. He'd have to leave the area and start all over again. As bad as Blake had hurt me, I couldn't help but feel guilty.

That durn Janine. I needed to send her a text and tell her to stop praying. I hadn't expected her prayers to work so quickly and she was messing up my plan. I needed her to stop bothering God so He would stop bothering me. At least until Roxie got to step number ten.

I waited until everyone left and finally made my way home. I pulled a Lean Cuisine out of the refrigerator for Sunday dinner. It wasn't like I was trying to lose weight, but frozen dinners were the cheapest way to go and I was all about saving money these days.

I spent the rest of the afternoon watching movies on Lifetime and ignoring calls and text messages from Janine. She said she thought she would have seen me at church and wanted me to go out to eat. She also wanted to know if I had talked to God about everything that was going on and if He had answered. And she wanted me to know that she was still praying for me. I refused to answer her. The guilt from the church services was bothering me enough. I didn't need Janine to make it worst.

What was really difficult was ignoring God. I could almost feel Him tapping me on the shoulder, wanting to talk to me but I just sat there on the couch, pretending I didn't feel Him or hear Him.

Me and God had a funny relationship. I remembered Roxie's attitude from my early years of growing up. It wasn't that she didn't believe in God. In fact, I think she believed in God so much that she thought it was best that she stay far away from Him because of all the dirt she did on a daily basis. So in the early years, we never went to church, never prayed and the only Bible in the house was the big dusty one on the living room table.

When Roxie left, my grandmother made sure I was in the church every time the doors opened. She figured she hadn't done a good job of raising Roxie and wanted to make sure I turned out differently. After Roxie left, she made a lot of really strict rules about music, television and movies, boys, everything. In her eyes, the last thing I needed was to end up being a rank heathen like my mother.

I really enjoyed going to church as a teenager, probably because I had lots of friends in my youth group and choir. There were a couple women in the church that must have felt sorry for me and took me under their wing as a daughter, especially since Grandma was always working. So I enjoyed the fellowship of a church family.

But God? I had to admit that I always kinda kept Him at arm's distance. I couldn't understand why a God who was supposed to be so loving and so good could let bad things happen to me. How could it be that I never even met my father? That my mother honestly admitted to me and my grandmother that she didn't even know who he was? How was it that my mother who I adored and loved to spend every waking minute with could just leave me like she never loved me?

Me and Roxie used to have the most fun. We'd spend every Saturday in the kitchen with Grandma, cooking Sunday dinner and the best desserts you ever wanted to taste. That's how I learned to make German Chocolate Cake. That was my favorite, but I could bake any cake or pie better than anyone I knew. Even the old mothers in the church.

When Roxie would get in from her late night escapades, she'd climb into the bed we shared and tickle me until I woke up. She'd tell me all the stories of what she'd done. I'd be excited and horrified at the same time. I'd always swear I'd never grow up and be like her. But at the same time, she fascinated me.

Every day after school, she'd be waiting for me. We'd walk home and stop at the park. She pushed me on the swing forever, and then we'd slide down the slide and she'd ride on the merry-go-round with me, even though she was a grown woman. When we got to the house, she'd do most of my homework so I wouldn't get yelled at when Grandma came home from work.

Every once in a while, Roxie would get a job and I wouldn't see her as much. It never lasted for more than a few months though. She always found some reason to quit or got in a fight with someone and got fired. Or got caught sleeping with someone and had to leave before she got fired.

Whenever she wasn't up under some man, it was always me and her. Having fun, laughing and getting into all kinds of trouble that my grandmother said would kill her before her time.

Until Mr. St. James came along. Then I started seeing her less and less. When it seemed like they were getting serious, she'd try to include me on their dates, but he always acted like he didn't want me around. One night when he brought her home, I heard them arguing in the living room about how he never wanted children – not his own, and especially not any other man's.

The next day when I woke up, she was gone. I didn't see her again until my grandmother's funeral.

So even though I knew it was important to do right and serve God, I never really got over the fact that He took away the two women I really needed in my life at important times in my life. I served Him because it was the right thing to do, but I didn't take it overboard like Janine. All that praying and helping people was too much to ask. I figured as long as I didn't commit any of the big sins, me and God should be straight.

I flipped through the channels trying to drown out a nagging realization. Not only did I need to forgive Blake and Roxie. Maybe I needed to forgive God too.

# *thirteen*

B lake's day off turned into almost a whole week. I guess he couldn't bear the thought of being at work while he was wondering whether he had HIV or not. I knew he had to be scared out of his mind. I couldn't imagine waiting and wondering every day until those test results came back. I called him and texted him every once in a while during the week with work questions. He'd send brief answers. I probably should have been the caring fiancé and tried to press him and find out what was wrong. For real though, I was enjoying the break from being around him all the time.

While he was gone, I caught up on things at work. It was peaceful in the office, and I realized I actually liked my job. I just didn't want to be there with him. Hopefully I could find something similar in another law office somewhere.

On Thursday afternoon, Blake called, his voice sounding completely different than it had all week. "Sabrina dear, how are you?"

"Fine, Blake. Are you okay?"

"I am absolutely wonderful. Never better." I don't think I had ever heard him sound so happy. He must have gotten a call from his doctor's office and found out that his tests were negative.

"Is everything okay at the office?" he asked. "Sorry to have left you all week, but...it just couldn't be helped. I'll be back tomorrow."

My stomach sank. I considered calling in sick the next day to avoid him.

"You have to let me make it up to you. Dinner tomorrow night at my place?"

Ugh. The last thing I felt like was spending an evening with Blake. "Of course, dear. That sounds wonderful. Should I order something to be delivered?"

"I'll have Bella cook something for us before she leaves. See you about eight?"

I crossed my eyes and let out a deep breath, but made my voice cheerful. "I'm looking forward to it."

I hung up and thought about how his voice sounded. He was almost...kind. I wonder if spending the week at home thinking he might have a scary disease had made him think about himself and maybe have some sort of change of heart about the way he'd treated me and his other women.

A few minutes later, Paris approached my desk with her gossip face on.

"Hey Paris, what's up?" I really didn't want to hear what she had to say, but it was honestly the only way to get rid of her. I rearranged several briefs on my desk and opened a file on my computer. Maybe if I looked busy she'd spill the info quick and then go away.

"Nothing. Just came by to say hi."

That was her technique when I was supposed to beg the information out of her. "Okay then. Hi, Paris. Thanks for stopping by, but as you can see, I have tons of work to do."

"For now," she said, baiting me.

"What do you mean, 'for now'?"

"Nothing." She pressed her lips together with a too serious look on her face.

"Paris, I'm not in the mood. If you have something to say, just say it. Otherwise I'd really like to get back to work."

She looked offended. "You're being pretty rude for a person that's about to be unemployed."

Now she really had my attention. I turned away from my computer monitor and stood, facing her. "What are you talking about?"

She smirked. "Come on. You know what's been going on around here. Wonderboy has completely fallen apart. First that fiasco with those...things from that...store. And then the magazines. And then blowing that huge Peterson account. And now rumor has it that something happened Sunday at his church that makes his integrity questionable. And you know in this business, integrity is everything."

My mouth went dry and my hands started to shake. Apparently I was finally giving Paris the reaction she came here for. "All I'm saying is, instead of planning to move to that fancy partner office, you may want to start looking for a new job. Because your man's days here are numbered."

My eyes flew open.

"Please, Sabrina. You think I don't know?" Paris rolled her eyes and walked away.

Those guilty feelings flooded me again. I looked up at the ceiling, wanting to talk to God but feeling so awful about what we had done that I couldn't think of anything to say. I had to tell Blake what was going on. If he knew what was coming, maybe there was some way he could salvage his position at the law firm.

More importantly, I needed to talk to Roxie. I never knew when the revenge next step would be executed and I needed to stop it before it started.

# fourteen

Roxie seemed all too happy when I called her and told her we needed to talk. She was busy that evening but said we could get together the next day. I decided to call in sick since Blake would be back in the office. If my days at the company were numbered, I might as well use up all my sick time.

When I arrived at Roxie's place, I stood outside her door for a few minutes, not sure what to do. I wanted to tell her to end the whole thing. Even though Blake treated me – us – so badly, I didn't want to go a step further with her ten steps to revenge. I would say thanks for all her help and say goodbye.

After she opened the door, Roxie studied my face as I stepped into the foyer and just stood there without talking.

"What?"

"Nothing." Roxie turned slowly and walked into her kitchen, indicating with a nod of her head that I was supposed to follow her. She had on a beige lounging outfit with an apron tied around her. "Come on in the kitchen."

Just stepping into the kitchen with her brought back memories. Sweet memories. Her kitchen was sleek and modern with stainless steel appliances, black marble countertops and dark, hardwood floors. There were a few things that didn't quite fit the art deco décor. There was a set of country looking cookie jar canisters, just like the ones we used to have in grandma's kitchen in our old house in Annapolis. The old spice rack, bread box and cast iron skillets looked exactly like the ones grandma used to have.

I saw Roxie watching me take it all in. "Just a few touches can make it feel like home, huh?"

I nodded without saying anything. There was a big picture of grandma on the wall over the eat-in kitchen table. I stared at her for a minute, feeling the pain of losing her all over again. Seemed like my life ended when she died. I had been lonely since the day I watched them lower her into the ground.

"Where'd you get that picture? All this stuff?"

"I took a few pictures when I left." Roxie looked around the kitchen. "Other stuff I've collected little by little over the years. Any time I saw something that reminded me of her...of you, I would pick it up."

I nodded.

"I know you think I left without looking back and without thinking about you two, but I didn't. You were always there with me. In my heart."

I didn't want to feel anything, but ever since Janine started praying, I couldn't seem to make my heart as hard or cold against Roxie. "So what's the plan for this evening?" Even though I wasn't as angry, I still didn't want to be all mushy with her.

She smiled. "We're gonna bake a cake. Just like old times." Her eyes twinkled. "You said Blake's favorite was German Chocolate, right?

I frowned. "Yeah. Why?"

She smiled that diabolical smile. "Because there's nothing like the sweet taste of revenge."

Roxie went to the cabinets and started pulling down ingredients. "Here, help me with this." She pulled out a large mixing bowl identical to the one that grandma used to bake all her cakes and pies with.

My eyes widened.

She laughed. "Brings back memories, huh?"

I nodded.

I started quietly sifting flour while Roxie creamed a few sticks of butter. I knew we were both remembering our baking Saturdays in the kitchen with grandma. She would teach us all her best recipes and we'd spend all day in the kitchen laughing, eating, listening to grandma's stories from when she was a little girl and hearing Roxie's tales of the life she would live when she left Annapolis.

"I guess you ended up with the life you always wanted, huh?"

Roxie looked up and a sad smile crossed her face. I knew she was reliving the same memories when she answered me without skipping a beat. "Yeah, I did everything I ever thought I wanted to do. But looking back, I missed out on what mattered most in life."

I measured out the baking powder and added it to the flour.

Roxie measured out cocoa powder and set it aside. "I always wondered what you were doing. Where you were. How your life had ended up. I know you don't believe me, but there wasn't a day that went by that I didn't think about you."

I greased and floured the three round cake pans Roxie had pulled out. Grandma was famous for making huge three layer cakes that melted in your mouth. I could never eat a whole piece. Blake would usually eat his entire slice and then finish off mine.

Roxie poured the batter into two of the pans and dropped them onto the counter a few times to get rid of any air bubbles. "Wanna taste?"

I smiled. "I'll lick the bowl when we're through."

"No bowl licking today. If you want a taste, you better get it now."

Roxie chuckled and I knew she was remembering how we fought over who would get to lick the bowl when we finished mixing our cakes. The smile left her face and she looked up at me. "I was so young and so not ready. That's all I can say, Sabrina."

I looked away. "Aren't you gonna pour the third pan?"

She raised her eyebrows. "Not quite yet. We need a special ingredient for the third layer." She disappeared from the kitchen and came back with a small brown bag. She reached in and pulled out a box.

I read the label and my eyes flew open. "Ex-lax? Oh my goodness, Roxie."

She laughed that deep hoarse laugh as she saw the shock on my face. "Didn't you say he had that big presentation tomorrow morning? This cake will be ready just in time for you to take it upstairs for your date tonight. You'll eat it with him so he won't be suspicious. Just don't eat the top layer."

I laughed for a second, but then felt that twinge of guilt. I didn't say anything for a few minutes and watched Roxie melt the Ex-lax and mix it with the remaining batter. She poured the mixture into the third cake pan and put all three pans in the oven.

"Now, you go into my bedroom. There's a box on the bed for you. Put that on and I'll be there in a few minutes after I clean up this mess."

I frowned at her. She smiled and shooed me away. "Just go. It's the room on the left."

I walked into Roxie's bedroom. It was a larger bedroom than I would have expected for a condo with a main area for the bed and nightstand and stuff and then a little sitting room off to the side. She had a large bed with a satiny red comforter covered with pillows. On the bed there was a large, white box.

I opened it and pulled out a beautiful red dress. I looked at the tag and saw it was a size 4. Roxie had bought me a dress? There were also some red pumps in the box, higher than I would have ever dreamed of wearing and some beautiful red and silver jewelry. I quickly slipped the dress on. It fit a lot closer than the clothes I usually wore and the clinginess of the material made me wonder how much of me I was showing. The fabric was rich and silky and I wondered how much Roxie could have paid for it. I sat on the bed for a second, remembering how much Roxie used to love to bring me the cutest outfits and dresses and shoes when we were growing up together.

I looked over into the sitting room and noticed a familiar book on a small nightstand. It was Grandma's old photo album that had gone missing the day Roxie left. I walked into the room and picked it up and started turning through the pages. There were lots of pictures of me at all different ages. There were pictures of grandma mixed in and several pictures of me and Roxie together.

As I turned further toward the end of the book, I realized there were pictures of me later in life, after Roxie had left. I gasped when I saw a picture of me dressed for my senior prom, of me graduating from high school, copies of my diploma, of me about to go on my first date.

"See, I was there, sorta..."

I whipped around to see Roxie standing behind me in the doorway. Her eyes glistened. "You look absolutely beautiful in that dress, Sabrina."

"Where...where did you get these pictures?"

Roxie walked over to stand next to me in her sitting room. "I took them when I left." She ran a finger over my prom and graduation pictures. "The rest your grandmother sent me. She mailed me packages every so often, all full of stuff about you."

My eyes fell on a little table in the corner. Perched on top was an old raggedy brown doll with one missing eye and stringy hair. I let out a deep breath. "Mimi?" I went over and picked up my favorite childhood toy. It had also disappeared when Roxie left. I was done playing with dolls by that time so it didn't bother me that much.

"Sorry. I took her. I just needed something..." Roxie looked down at the floor. A tear trickled down her cheek. "I slept with that doll every night. No telling how many of my tears are soaked into her clothes. Mr. St. James fussed about it every night but I told him it was all I had left of my daughter and if the doll left, I left."

I swallowed hard. Part of me was angry. But what I felt the most was pity. Staring into her eyes I realized that in her running off to chase her dreams, Roxie had lost what it took her too long to realize mattered the most.

She wiped her face. "Come on. We gotta get you ready for your date." She led me into her bathroom. It was huge with a shower and marble Jacuzzi tube and a double bowl vanity. She sat me down on an antique chair in front of her large mirror and pulled a make-up palette out of a drawer. She set it on the vanity and stood behind me, putting her hands on my shoulders.

We both stared at our reflections, looking at our own face in the other's. Another tear trickled down Roxie's face. She reached for the bun at the back of my neck and pulled out the pins that kept it in place. "You have such beautiful hair. Always did." She tousled it a little and made it look wild. She took a large brush and began pulling it through my hair without saying a word. More tears poured down her cheeks.

I didn't want to say a word. I felt years of anger, hatred, and bitterness pouring out of me into a puddle at my feet. I felt a sting on my cheek and realized I had tears flowing as well.

"Now how am I supposed to put you on some makeup with your face all wet?"

I smiled through my tears and wiped my face. "I don't like a whole lot of make-up."

"You don't need a lot. Just the basics."

After she finished my make-up and hair, Roxie stood me in front of the mirror. "Such a beautiful girl." She put her hands on my shoulders. "I would apologize a thousand times if I thought it would make a difference." She turned me to her and grabbed both my hands. "I missed so much, Sabrina. Please don't make me miss more. I…I want to be in your life again. Even if you can't see me as your mother, can we at least be friends?"

I stood there with my mouth open. I didn't know what to say. Could I forgive her? Could I let her be a part of my life?

My cell phone rang. We both stood there frozen for a few seconds and then she picked it up off the counter and handed it to me. "I'm sure it's him. What time are you supposed to be upstairs?"

"Eight o'clock." I looked down at the phone. It was Janine's number. I didn't answer it.

"I better get those cakes out of the oven and into the fridge for a second so they can be cool enough for me to put the icing on. Go ahead and put some powder on and meet me in the kitchen." Roxie gave my hair one last pat and walked out of the bathroom.

A few seconds later, a text message came through from Janine.

*Just wanted to let you know that I was praying for you. God is going to give you the strength to for-*

*give. Promise me that when you do, you'll share your Mommy with me. Love you forever.*

I sat there looking at myself in the mirror. I looked more like Roxie than I did myself. And I had to admit that I did feel beautiful. In spite of myself, I had turned out more like her than I ever wanted to be.

I walked out into the kitchen as Roxie was taking the cake pans out of the ovens. She set the Ex-lax layer away from the other two layers so as not to get them mixed up.

"I can't do it anymore, Roxie."

She looked up at me. "Do what?"

"This." I looked down at the cake pans. "This... revenge thing. It was really fun at first because I was hurt really bad, but now...it's not so fun anymore."

"Okay..." Roxie gave me a questioning look.

"I've been angry and hateful for so long and now...I don't want to be angry and hateful anymore. I just want to...forgive."

Roxie looked at me with hope in her eyes. "Forgive?"

I nodded.

She reached out to me and I walked into her arms. We stood there hugging and crying for what felt like forever. I didn't have any tears left. And when we finished, I didn't have any hate left either.

"I love you, Sabrina. Always have." Roxie whispered into my hair. She pulled back from our embrace to look at me. "And I'm so sorry I messed up. I was so young and so..."

"I forgive you, Roxie. I forgive you."

We hugged again. When we pulled away, Roxie wiped my face and looked me in the eye. "You sure you're through? With this whole Blake thing? Five steps is enough revenge for you?"

I laughed and nodded. "Yeah, five steps is more than enough."

Roxie smiled. She picked up the Ex-lax cake and turned it over into the trash can. "Okay, it's done."

Her cell phone vibrated. She picked it up and looked at the screen. "Well, now ain't that something. We mighta thrown that cake away too fast."

I frowned.

"This joker just sent me a text saying he wants to come by for a quickie before his eight o'clock meeting tonight. Says he's on his way down in ten minutes. Ain't that something?"

I was surprised that I didn't feel even a flicker of anger in my heart. I shrugged my shoulders.

Her eyes twinkled and she picked up the phone and typed a text message.

"What did you tell him?" The look in her eye made me ask.

"I told him to come on down. I figured if we're gonna end it, we might as well end with a bang."

# fifteen

Roxie disappeared into her bedroom and ree-merged moments later in a sexy, red dress of her own. "Have a seat in my bedroom. I'll call for you in a second." She winked and shooed me into her room.

I sat in the sitting room, flipping through the photo album. As I looked at the pictures of me, Roxie and grandma, for the first time, I felt some peace about us all. It seemed like the huge rock of hate that I had carried around on my shoulders for years was gone. I felt light and free. Brand new.

A few minutes later, I heard a knock on Roxie's front door. I heard her shoes clacking through the foyer and I went and stood behind her cracked bedroom door so I could hear.

Roxie's voice was low and sexy. "Well, hey baby. Why the long face? You okay?"

I could hardly hear Blake's voice as he mumbled something low.

"Well, come on in and tell Mama all about it. Can't nothing be that bad that a little lovin' can't fix it."

Their voices moved closer and I figured they must be sitting on the couch in the living room. I could hear Blake loud and clear. "I've had the worst few weeks of my life. I got called into a meeting today and found out I didn't make partner. From the way they sounded, I may even lose my job. I can't figure out who it was, but somebody in my company deliberately sabotaged me."

My heart beat faster as guilt and regret rose up in me. We had cost Blake his partnership.

"And this awful thing happened in church this Sunday and now I've been ostracized by all my friends and I've lost important social connections."

"I'm so sorry, Baby, but you know you got me."

*Forgive me, Lord. I didn't mean to destroy the man's life.* We had waited too late to stop our plan for revenge. I would have to find some way to apologize to Blake.

"And then my assistant called in sick today. I think she knows with everything going on at the job that my days there are numbered. She's probably out interviewing somewhere else."

"You don't know that. Maybe she was really sick. You always talk about how dedicated she is."

"She *was*. Lately, she's not been performing up to speed. In fact she's gotten downright lazy and useless." Blake's voice got louder and I could just imagine the angry look on his face. "I took her on when she was a lowly secretary. I've made her what she is today and she has the nerve to leave me? I mean, I've helped her grow personally and professionally. You should have seen her before I got to her. An absolute mess – a silly little girl with no experience or people skills. She didn't even know how to dress properly. Now she's the best in the office. They'll probably fire me and fight over who gets to keep her."

"Hmmmm..." I heard Roxie say. I could tell she was biting her tongue. So much for me feeling sorry for him.

Blake's voice rose. "I'll see about that. I can ruin her name at the law firm and then give her horrible recommendations wherever she tries to go."

Roxie's voice was a little tight. "Now why would you do that, honey? That girl's been good to you. You might have helped her, but she helped you too. You told me she took you to a whole new level in the company."

"Yeah, but what good did it do me? I didn't make partner. The whole point was for me to make partner. Now that it didn't happen, she was just a waste of time."

Roxie didn't say anything, but I knew she was thinking about rescuing that cake out of the trash can. I wasn't. Even though Blake was saying those hateful things, I was through. I didn't want to hate anyone ever again for the rest of my life.

"Anyway, I didn't come here to talk about her or any of other stuff. I came to spend some time with you before this meeting. You act right and I might cancel the meeting. It's not that important anyway." I heard the couch shifting a little and wondered how far Roxie was going to take this.

Blake's voice sounded low and soft. "Roxanne, you know how I feel about you. You mean the world to me. You've been there for me through all of this. I know we haven't been seeing each other that long but...well, everything that's happened lately has made me realize how much you mean to me. Since my life has completely gone to hell, we should do something crazy. Roxanne, will you marry me?"

I gritted my teeth and clenched my fists. Before I could get good and angry, Roxie let out that laugh of hers, low and throaty, strong and sexy. She laughed for a good while before Blake finally said something. "What's so funny?"

"Now honey, that's the craziest thing I've heard in a long time. Tell you what. Before we get married, there's something you should know about me."

"It doesn't matter. There's nothing you could tell me that would change my mind."

"Okay. In that case, I have a daughter."

"A child? You have a child? But surely she's grown and on her own, right?"

"Of course."

"Then why should that matter?"

"I'll let you decide." Roxie called out, "Sweetie, come on out here and meet your soon-to-be stepdaddy."

All the color drained from Blake's face when I walked into the living room. He jumped out of Roxie's arms off the couch and stood squared off. Roxie stood and put her hands on her hips. Blake looked at her and then at me and then at her and then at me. "You...you're..."

He walked around the couch to where I was and faced me. He was staring at me like he'd never seen me before and it took me a second to remember the hair, make-up and sexy red dress I was wearing.

I put my hands on my hips like Roxie. "Hi, Blakey." I looked down at my watch. "We still on for eight o'clock?"

"Sabrina, what are you doing here? Why are you..." He looked me up and down and then turned to Roxie again. "Your daughter?"

Roxie nodded and smiled. "Ain't she just beautiful? Now that's who you should be asking to marry you." She smirked.

Blake moved back from me to a neutral position between the two of us. "How long have you…"

"How long have we known about you and your lying, cheating ways?" Let me see…" Roxie stroked her chin like she was thinking. "Christine let us know about three weeks ago."

Blake's mouth dropped open and his eyes widened. "Christine?"

We both nodded. Roxie continued. "Yes, honey. Christine. And I have to tell you, Amber and Shaquetta weren't too happy about it either. We all took it kinda bad. But I can honestly say – we're all feeling better now."

Blake turned bright red and I could see the anger boiling up in him. "You…it was all of you? You all…did this to me?"

We both stood there, allowing everything to register in his brain.

"How could you do this to me? You've destroyed my life." Blake clenched his fists and walked toward Roxie. His breath was ragged and fast. I was almost afraid of what he would do to her.

She held up a hand. "Watch yourself now. You don't want to get cut, honey." Roxie smiled but her face was stone cold serious. "And I *will* cut you."

Blake had the good sense to back up off her. He turned to me. "Sabrina, how could you do this? I thought you loved me."

I laughed, sounding almost like Roxie when I did. "I thought you loved me too, Blake. See how it feels when you find out the truth?"

His eyes hardened. "You destroyed me and now I'm gonna destroy you. You'll never work in this city again. By the time I'm finished with you –"

In one move, Roxie stepped up in Blake's face, in front of me. "Now you *really* better watch yourself. Everything that happened to you was my doing. Not hers. She came over here and asked me to stop. You see, Roxie always plots out ten steps to revenge. My sweet little daughter here got nervous at five." Roxie leaned up so close to Blake's face, she could have kissed him. "You do anything...and I mean anything to hurt my daughter and I'll start all over again from step one. By the time I'm done with you, you'll never work anywhere in this country again. And you might just find yourself in jail. Or worse."

Roxie pointed a finger and jabbed it in his chest. "You hurt my daughter again and I'll make sure you never stop hurting. Now I suggest you get yourself out of here and forget you ever knew me. When you get to work on Monday, you pick the best lawyer in that firm and you give them a glowing recommendation about Sabrina and make sure they take her on. Right before you turn in your resignation. And if anything bad ever happens to her, I don't care if it's ten years from now, I'm coming after you. And this time I won't be stopped until I'm done."

Blake pressed his lips tight together.

"And the next time you decide you want to run some women, I want you to remember Roxie, hear?"

Blake turned on his heels and stormed toward the foyer. After he slammed the door, Roxie burst out into laughter. I just stood there. She walked over and took my hands.

"You okay, sweetie?"

I nodded. "Yeah. As long as I stay on your good side." We both laughed. She took me in her arms and I let her hug me. I squeezed her real tight and said, "Thanks, Roxie."

"Anything, anytime." She stepped away from me and said. "Well, I guess since you don't have your dinner date, you'll be going on home?"

I smiled and took her by the hand. "I thought I might stay around. And eat my favorite cake with my Mama."

A Piece of Revenge

by

Rhonda McKnight

Tashmin,
Love you "Sistah!"
Enjoy Tamara's journey
to peace.
BLESSINGS,
Rhonda

# *one*

I downshifted the gear and maneuvered my car into the left lane on I-10. I couldn't get downtown fast enough. "Four dollars and eighty-three cents." The thought of the balance in my bank account gave me a six hundred horsepower burst of adrenaline that not even a Lamborghini could match. I wasn't driving a sports car, not even close, so I had to use my good old "Tamera Watson" foot pressure on the gas pedal to push my late model, "need service and new tires", Honda Accord just above the sixty-five mile per hour speed limit. Dang computer glitches. They had robbed me of my joy this morning. I wanted to see the balance the account had grown to. I wanted to celebrate the clearing of the final deposits I'd made from the corporate benefactors who were subsidizing The Micah Center, my dream.

The Micah Center, named for the biblical prophet who spoke up for the little man, was an inner-city community center for kids; the ones who wandered the streets after school and on weekends. The ones looking for someplace to go and someplace to be productive that could not find one. Young lives waiting to be wasted in the drug infested, crime infested streets of south Phoenix. Lives like that of my younger brother who was serving the last few months of a ten year stint for bank robbery in an Arizona state penitentiary. I closed my eyes for a second to the pain that ten years had bought me, but I could not close my heart to my brother's words. "I didn't have anything else to do," Todd replied when our grandmother asked him why? Why after all she'd sacrificed to raise us after our mother died, why did he do something so foolish? *Nothing to do.* I shuddered and blinked back tears. My brother's life had been stolen, but I was determined that I would give some child something to do. Unfortunately, Phoenix Federal Bank was robbing me of the anticipation of that; them and their antiquated online banking system.

I'd tried to resolve the problem by logging out, refreshing the webpage and logging back in to see if things had miraculously been fixed in the two minute span of time it took to do all three, but they had not. The Micah Foundation still had less than five dollars in the account. I'd picked up the phone, dialed the customer service number and proceeded to push the series of numbers I needed from my account I.D. to the last four of my social. All to be told the bank was experiencing extremely high contact volume and to call back later. They didn't even let me hold. But then I figured the high contact volume was probably due to the fact that their computers had gone crazy and moved everybody's money around while we were asleep. No matter, I'd be there in less than five minutes. Well, that was if Miss Daisy would move to the right. I groaned. I downshifted again and moved back into the center lane.

I wasn't ordinarily this impatient on the road, but I had taken the day off from work to be productive, not downtown. I had bills to pay. Invoices that had been waiting for the corporate funds to become available. We could have taken care of the bills already, but Leon had insisted we wait.

*"No baby. Let's hold off until all the money is in the account. Don't you want to look at it? Don't you want to see the balance when it's at its highest?"*

He'd reminded me that vision was visual, and I'd acquiesced. I shivered just thinking about the pre-bill paying celebration we'd had that night. A smile curved my lips, and a flutter filled my belly. "Ooh, that man," I whispered into the emptiness of the car. *Vision.* He had enough for the both of us. That was one of the things I loved about him. He always convinced me to think big – bigger than I dared to. So against my normal operating code, I agreed to hold off on paying the vendor's down payments.

"They'll wait a few weeks," Leon had said and wait they had. Today I wanted to call them all and inform them their checks were in the mail. But I couldn't yet, because Phoenix Federal was messing up. I rolled my eyes in irritation at the driver in front of me, moved into the far right lane and made the quick exit off the interstate for Seventh Street. I ran right into a mini traffic jam. I hated coming downtown. *Maybe we should consider another bank*, I thought, reaching for my cell phone. I'd have to run that by Leon. I knew he preferred Federal, because he said they had excellent customer service, but I had had a small problem with a check not clearing before and now this computer thing was huge in my opinion. I didn't like logging on and finding one hundred and eighty thousand dollars missing from my account. I pressed the speed dial number for Leon's cell phone. He'd left so early this morning, I'd barely had time to kiss him let alone tell him the great idea I'd had for the center's opening day contest. The call went to voicemail. I sighed, put the phone down and waited until the traffic moved.

I exited my car and made rapid steps to the entrance of the bank. I barely escaped being knocked over by a man who was rushing to get through the door. He looked irate and I wondered if he had balance error, too. I waved at one of the men I knew to be an assistant branch manager. He'd helped me to complete the refinance on my house.

"Ms. Watson, good morning." The bank manager stuck out his hand as I approached.

"Good morning –," I stole a glance at his name badge. "Ken, I have a problem that I'm sure you're aware of." He raised his eyebrows like he had no idea what I was talking about. "With the online bank system." I threw my free hand up in a dramatic flair of frustration. "My account balance is incorrect."

Ken shook his head, let my hand go and ushered me into a glass encased cubicle a few feet away. "Let's see what's going on." I took a plush wing chair and observed as Ken clicked on the keyboard of the computer in front of him. "Your account number?"

"It's my business account. Tamera and Leon Watson for the Micah Foundation." I gave him the twelve numbers

I'd already committed to memory. Ken typed some more, gave his long, thin nose an exaggerated twist and turned the huge thirty-inch monitor toward me. I stared for a second. I saw something now that I had not seen on my home computer, because it didn't give very much information. The balance was still four dollars and eighty-three cents, but there was a debit for one hundred and eighty thousand dollars. My stomach lurched. "That's what I mean. The hundred and eighty thousand dollars, where is it? It's supposed to be in the account. I was waiting for the last sixty-thousand dollars to clear last night, but the other hundred and twenty had already been cleared and I shouldn't have a debit."

Ken coughed and did some more typing. "Well, Ms. Watson, you withdrew the funds." My stomach lurched again. I felt like I had sucked in a room full of bad air. *Withdrew the funds.* That was crazy. Ken was looking crazy. I cleared my throat and started my count to ten to stop the *spirit of cuss* that was fighting to come over me. Ken spoke and interrupted me at five. "The transaction was this morning, Ms. Watson. A check was posted against the account and one hundred eighty thousand dollars in funds were withdrawn."

I shook my head. "That's not possible." I think I said it. I wasn't sure. The room was shrinking. I felt lightheaded.

"It was taken in cash." Ken's voice was distorted like he was talking into one of those voice alerting devices. "I see the account was set up as an either/or signature account. Maybe Mr. Watson can explain." Ken was giving me one of those sympathy looks, the kind reserved for people whose heads turned into large lollipops with the word SUCKER written in red.

Leon, of course, he must have…"I'll call my husband." My legs were weak and my stomach had done a somersault, but I managed to stand. There had to be a reasonable explanation. I just couldn't imagine what it might be at this second. "I appreciate your time." I pretended to look for something in my purse to avoid extending my sweaty palm to Ken.

He seemed to sense my anxiety. "Please let me know if I can be of any assistance to you." He walked around the desk and reached into his jacket pocket for a business card. I took it, gave him a weak smile and turned on shaky legs to walk away from him. I reached into my bag for my phone and dialed Leon's number. It went to voice mail again. I cursed under my breath and ended the call. He did tell me he had a meeting. He must not be out yet. I dialed again, this time leaving a message, "Hey, baby, it's me. I've just left the bank and I really need you to call me. I wanted to pay the bills today so…" I hesitated. "Just call me."

I took the steps to exit the bank with less assurance than I had taken to enter it. I climbed into my car and heaved a few deep breaths in and out before starting the ignition. "It's okay Tamera. Leon's a leader." I knew he had made some type of decision that was for our benefit. "He just made it without me. Which as the head of our home he was entitled to do," I said and looked to the left. The driver in the car next to me was staring at me like I was a loon, because I was talking to myself. I pulled out of the parking space and maneuvered the short distance to the interstate. I debated going to Leon's office, but in the end decided to go home. Whatever Leon had decided was a good thing. My husband was a smart businessman. Everything was going to be fine. I tried to convince myself of that, but somehow the nagging in the pit of my gut told me that something was horribly wrong.

# *two*

"**Y**ou what?" Erin Young flew out of her chair and came to stand in front of me.

"I told you, it was a joint account. I'm not thinking about that right now. What if something happened to him?"

"Something like what?" Erin yelled. "He told you he was going to the office, not the bank. He told you he had meetings today and the secretary said they haven't seen him. You've been calling his cell all day and getting voicemail and you're thinking something could have happened to him?"

I pushed my body deeper into the sofa cushion and looked beyond Erin's angry form. Through the mini blind slots, I could see the sun setting over the desert in the horizon. I was starting to get a headache and Erin was making it worse. I took a deep breath and let it carry my weak protest. "Leon wouldn't take our money."

Erin guffawed and shook her head. "Leon didn't take *our* money. He took your money."

I rolled my eyes. My husband was not a thief. I was seriously concerned about him and here this girl was talking crazy. "Erin, just stop. I'm really worried about him. He could have been kidnapped or robbed. You know, somebody could have made him take that money out of the bank. Somebody who knew what we were planning. We did announce the center's opening plans in the paper. We did talk about the money we'd gotten from the grants. This was public information."

Erin was shaking her head.

"What?" I asked. "I know Leon, Erin. Somebody is keeping him from calling. Something bad went down."

"So if you think somebody took him then why'd you call me instead of the police?"

"Because you're my best friend. I'm scared and I thought you could help me make the call. I didn't want to go through it alone."

Erin shook her head. "Let me get this straight. You called me to help you get the courage to call the police to report your husband missing, or kidnapped after he took one hundred and eighty thousand dollars from your joint account. I, who you knew would say exactly what I'm saying right now, that the low-life stole your money."

My cell phone rang. I made a desperate lunge for it and pushed one of the buttons without even looking at the caller I.D. "Leon." The voice on the other end came through a computerized system that advised me to press the number "one" to hear about a great price on an extended auto warranty. I wanted to cry. *Where was my husband?* I put down the phone.

"I can't believe you had all that money mixed together and in an account that either one of you had full access to," Erin ranted. "Don't they still have joint signature accounts in banks?"

Of course they did. I didn't dignify her rhetorical question with an answer. I couldn't believe it was after eight p.m., and Leon hadn't called.

"You've only been married for five months, Tamera. You didn't even know him that long before you married him."

I rolled my eyes and popped to my feet. I moved to the kitchen, pulled the refrigerator open, and removed a can of ginger-ale. Maybe it would help my stomach stop turning. I hadn't eaten all day, and I wasn't feeling well. My nerves were on edge.

I looked back at Erin who was now in an arms crossed, feet tapping frenzy.

I tried to block out her negative words, but I was having a war in my own head about the whole thing. My heart said, "you love him, you trust him", but my logical mind said, "money's gone, he's missing". The logical side of me was winning, but my heart was putting up a good fight. "I'm telling you, I know him." I reentered the family room and returned to my seat. "We have the same dream to open the center. Something is wrong."

"Yeah, there's something wrong alright. You've been reading way too many romance novels, girlfriend. " Erin flopped down on the sofa, pulled the cordless phone from its base and handed it to me. "It's time to call the police."

# three

The telephone call to the police was a waste of time. Leon had been gone for less than twenty-four hours, so they refused to take a missing person report, but they were more than happy to refer me to an attorney. I didn't need a lawyer. I needed an investigation. Leon was a big man, almost six foot two, two hundred twenty pounds, but even a big man could be overpowered by a team of thugs. Besides I knew there was no way Leon stole from me. He wasn't a thief. He was missing and probably in danger. I shuddered at the thought. I climbed into my bed and laid there, body in knots, heart frozen all night.

I was finally able to officially report Leon missing at noon on Saturday. The policeman who took the report all but snickered in my face when I'd told him the circumstances surrounding his disappearance. "Okay, let me recap the details." The red, pock faced cop moved the form he'd been writing in around on the desk. "You think your husband has been kidnapped or in an accident."

I nodded.

"The two of you hadn't talked about the money, hadn't agreed to move it to another bank, or stick it in a crate under the mattress."

I nodded again.

"Okay." He whistled low and hard. After making a few more notes, he asked, "Did he by any chance pack?"

"Pack? No." I shook my head. *This was ridiculous.* "I don't understand the question. If he'd packed would I be here saying he was missing? His clothes are still in the closet."

The police officer leaned back a bit. A smug expression came over his face before he asked, "Did your husband own anything that was really valuable to him? Photographs, books, a stamp collection, game ball? Anything that'd he'd never leave without?"

My mouth dropped open. Leon owned an autographed Michael Jordan Chicago Bulls championship game jersey. He kept it in a special fireproof case in the back of the closet. It was worth more than three thousand dollars. He would never leave it behind. I met the cop's eyes. "Well, yes, he owns a jersey. It's worth a lot to him."

"You let me know if it's missing. I've got everything I need to put out the report."

"It's not missing." I was emphatic. "Once I confirm that, will you put out an all points bulletin?" I'd heard that on television. I wasn't even sure what it meant, but it seemed urgent.

"You check for that jersey. If it's there, I'll look for him myself." He winked.

I wanted to snatch him across the counter. Did he think this mess was funny? That my husband might be in a ditch somewhere was funny? "I don't like your attitude, Officer," I sneered. "I assure you I'll be putting in a complaint to your superior."

He shoved the papers for my report in a file, turned his back to me and threw words over his shoulder. "We'll be in touch, Mrs. Watson."

But they weren't in touch. The weekend came and went. I'd called Leon's cell phone at least fifty times. There was no more room in the voicemail. I couldn't believe that I hadn't heard from him, and I was really starting to think I was being a fool for believing something had happened to him.

I stood outside his closet door. When I returned from the police department, I didn't check for the jersey. I wasn't going to dignify the cop's ridiculous insinuation about Leon's character by actually looking for it. But now it was seventy-two hours since I'd last seen my husband. I had to know. I had to know, but I couldn't bring myself to turn the doorknob to his closet. I was too afraid. I was afraid that if I found Leon's jersey that someone had hurt my husband and afraid that if I didn't find it, he had hurt me. But I had to know. If I was going to call the police and demand they step up their search for Leon, I had to be able to answer the question the police officer had posed to me. *"Did your husband own anything that was really valuable to him? Anything that'd he'd never leave without?"*

Leon worshipped that game jersey. He told me he was planning to have it framed, and he'd hang it in his office in the center. That is after we had the security system installed. He would never leave it behind. I shook my head. "This is crazy," I whispered to myself. "Leon did not steal our money." I turned the knob and pulled the door open. I bolstered confidence and stepped into the long walk-in closet, but something hit me in my spirit. It was a blow like a baseball bat against my chest that sucked the wind from my lungs. I had to fight to keep the bile down and work to move my feet, because I already knew without reaching the area where the jersey was kept, that it was gone.

# four

I called in sick from work. Not only was I sick, but it was time to do what the police had suggested and talk to an attorney. I had a serious problem. Not only was the money from the sale of my grandmother's house gone. All ninety thousand dollars of it, but so was the money we'd raised at the neighborhood rally and eighty thousand dollars I'd gotten from the corporations who'd given me grant funds. Only ten thousand of the money was actually Leon's and God only knows who he'd stolen that from.

"I'm trying to make sure I'm hearing you right." I shifted in my seat and blinked against tears that were burning my eyes. "You're telling me that there's nothing I can do?"

The attorney was looking at me the same way Ken from the bank had looked at me, like I had a sucker for a head, or at least that's how I perceived her sad expression. "He has broken the law by stealing the corporate funds, but you'll have to find him first and prove he was the one that took and spent the money. He could just as easily say he removed the money for both of you."

I was getting more furious by the minute. "But he was the one who went to the bank."

"I know, but what happened to the money after that is your word against his. He could say you both agreed to take the money out. You'd have to show a trail that led to his having the money."

This was unbelievable. "His missing isn't a trail?"

"He's not really missing. He's only been gone a few days, Mrs. Watson."

"But he's not coming back. That jersey is proof that he's not coming back. He officially packed. It was just light." I sighed. This was beyond humiliating. This woman, the police officer and Erin could not believe I had been naïve enough to trust a man I hardly knew with all that money. What they didn't understand, was that I thought, really believed that I had met my soul mate. I believed that Leon loved me. I couldn't have been more stupid.

"I'm sorry I don't have better news," the attorney said. "Perhaps you can raise money some other way. They were matching grant funds, so you'd have to raise enough to equal the amount you received by the time you have to fiscally account for how you spent the money. You do have a year."

I stood on weak knees. A year. Was she kidding? I'd need more than that to come up with eighty thousand dollars. I had to get the money back. "What if I found my husband and found the money. I could take it back, couldn't I?"

"Mrs. Watson, I advise you to contact the police and let them handle this."

"Why? So they can tell me the same thing you just did? It was our money." I pulled the strap of my handbag from the arm of the chair and turned toward the door. "I appreciate your time." I left the office.

I was so screwed. I had not only been robbed of my grandparent's inheritance, but now I was going to have a legal problem if I didn't have eighty thousand dollars in a year.

"Leon, how could you do this?" I asked in the quiet of my automobile. I grabbed the steering wheel and gripped it with all my might. It was finally going to happen. The thing I'd been fighting all morning, all weekend really. The tears I'd been keeping down in my soul were finally going to fall.

# *five*

I walked into my house, kicked off my shoes and entered the small family room. More tears rolled down my cheeks. I'd had to cry without losing control as I'd driven home, but now that I was here there was no reason to hold back. I sobbed until I was hoarse and couldn't cry anymore. Not only was my husband gone, but so was my dream. The Micah Center had been stolen from me, stolen from the children I was trying to help.

"God, how could this happen? How could you allow him to steal the center? I thought this was your will. " God didn't answer me. I was beginning to wonder if He was listening. I had been praying all weekend for Leon to be okay, to not be hurt, for our money to not have been stolen, but in the end it had been. Stolen by the man I thought God sent to me to be my husband.

I picked myself up off the floor. It was time for some serious therapy. Oh yeah, a sistah needed to stretch out on the proverbial couch. I went into the kitchen, opened the refrigerator and reached in for a pint of chocolate fudge ice-cream. I removed a serving spoon from the silverware drawer, grabbed some napkins and headed

back to the family room. I don't care what anyone says, Sigmund Freud didn't have nothing on Ben and Jerry's.

I turned on the television and aside from a bunch of stupid talk shows, decorating shows and reruns of all the *Law and Order* franchises. There was nothing to watch. I wasn't used to being home in the middle of the day and when I was, I would spend my time reading everything I could about running a non-profit or grant writing, etc, etc, — all the things it took to take my dream to the next level.

I shoved a huge spoonful of ice-cream in my mouth to keep the scream from coming out. I blinked against new tears and put the television guide back up. I noticed a title for a show that seemed to match how I was feeling. *Snapped*. I'd never heard of it before, but it looked interesting. The guide listed this episode as "*A woman murders her husband when she finds out he's cheating on her.*"

"Okay, I'm feeling that," I said. An hour later I was done with the ice-cream, eating Oreos and watching the twelve p.m. episode of *Snapped*. "*A woman murders her husband and his children think she was a gold digger. They fight until they bring her to justice.*" One p.m. "*A woman murders her husband for insurance money.*" Two p.m., three p.m., four p.m. snap after snap after snap. It was a women gone wild murdering marathon. The pizza man came and went. So did the Chinese delivery man. Did this show ever end? There was an entire underworld of murdering, stealing wives and husbands out there. Apparently, I was lucky to be alive, because Leon was one of them.

I attempted to get dressed for work the next day, but I just couldn't. There was no way I was going to be able to concentrate, so I called my boss. "Hi Tracey, I hate to call in again, but I really think I have the flu." I knew I already sounded horrible, but I coughed for good measure.

"You do sound bad. Stay home. The last thing we need is you coming in here and infecting everyone. I know you've been running yourself ragged getting ready for the opening."

"Yeah, I have, but I'll make sure to get caught up before taking time off," I promised, knowing full well there would be no opening. No need to take any additional days after I finished grieving.

Tracey and I ended the call. I went in the kitchen and put some cut and bake cookies in the oven. They'd make a great breakfast. I was so bloated from eating sugar and salty food. I knew I was going to gain weight. I had a vision of my behind blowing up into a balloon every time I ate something, but I couldn't stop myself from eating and I didn't dare look at myself in the full length mirror. I was depressed enough. I just put on a big tee-shirt and crashed in front of the television.

Between the crazy movies on *Lifetime* and episodes of *Snapped* I had lots of drama to fill my time. But then there were the commercials. Those stupid cruise lines vacations with families and couples and happy housewife commercials that made me miss the one thing I wanted more than my precious Micah Center — a family of my own. I threw myself into the seat cushion and started bawling again. Leon and I were supposed to live happily ever after. We were supposed to have beautiful brown babies and raise them to be full of destiny and purpose. Our kids would literally turn the world upside down. We'd even tossed around strong, meaningful names for them. Didn't that mean anything to him? Had he been a phony or had he changed?

"Lies, deceit, murder, betrayal," the announcer on the television said. I stopped crying. It was time for the next episode of *Snapped*. "*A woman's baby is kidnapped by her ex-husband.*" This was going to be a trip. I settled in, watched with new enthusiasm, because this woman had done something that none of the other folks on *Snapped* did. She'd hired a team of private detectives. I sat up in my seat at the same time the oven was dinging to tell me to get my cookies. Why hadn't I thought of that? I went into the kitchen, pulled the tray from the oven and placed it on top of the stove. A private detective. They find people. Maybe one could find Leon.

I grabbed the phone book, wondering what it cost. I opened it to the yellow pages listings for private investigators. Empowered to take control over this mess, I placed a few calls. I got answering machine after answering machine. When I didn't get a machine I reached a receptionist who I imagined was filing her nails and chewing bubble gum. Were these guys legit? I let out a long sigh, went into my office with the phone book and plopped down into the chair. There were lots of them and I was in for the long haul on finding one.

I had not turned on my computer in days which was not like me. Big sign of depression, but I needed to know how much money I had to the penny. I signed on to my bank account, and then my credit card account. I had about two hundred dollars in cash. No surprise there, but I didn't realize how much I'd paid down my credit card. I had eighteen hundred dollars in available credit. I twisted my lips. "What were the chances I could find him with two thousand dollars?" I said, but then I shook off doubt. I knew he could be anywhere in the entire world, especially with nearly two hundred thousand dollars, but I had to try. I had to do something. I picked up the phone and called the next private investigator listed in the book. *Powers Investigations.* The voice on the other end of the phone was not a bubble gum chewing airhead. It was male and it definitely sounded powerful. It was strong, and sexy. He sounded black. Were brothers P.I.'s? I was about to find out.

"Hello, I need a consultation for a – I need to have someone – found," I choked out the words.

"That's what I do," the voice said. "But I don't do phone meetings."

"I know. None of you do," I replied, thinking about the response I'd gotten from the other detectives. "You're local, so I'll be there in twenty minutes if you can see me."

"Sure, I'm working on paperwork. I'd love to push it aside. Come right in." The voice was so welcoming.

I looked down at my ice-cream stained tee-shirt. Thought about the three days worth of butt funk I needed to wash off and the matted mess on top of my head. "Make that an hour."

# six

*Powers Investigations* was located in a small, two room space over a lawyer's office on a less than attractive street in downtown Chandler. I pushed the button for an elevator that looked like it had been installed by slaves. They were sorely in need of an upgrade. The office space did not get me excited about *Powers Investigations*. I hoped he was in the habit of passing some of the money he saved on office space to his customers, because I'd been quoted some hefty prices on the other calls.

The elevator creaked and croaked, and I finally made it to the second floor. I was relieved when the door opened. I was even more relieved when I found Hill Harper or rather, his taller even more handsome brother standing there. My voice left me.

"Ms. Watson." He reached his hand in, took mine. "Be careful. The step isn't even."

I looked down and saw that the elevator floor was not quite in line with the carpeted hallway I was exiting onto. I looked back up and time seemed to stop. He was staring. His soft, chestnut eyes had tiny flecks of green in the irises. They looked like topaz gemstones. The earlier apprehension left my body. It went back down to the first floor with the closing elevator.

"I'm Kemuel Powers. Most people call me Powers." He released my hand, which I needed him to do. A sistah was feeling really vulnerable, and the last thing I needed was to think Mr. Powers had superpowers or I'd be handing over my credit card hoping he'd rescue me. A good looking man had already beat me out of my money this month.

"Let's step into my office."

We moved about ten feet to a set of doors, passed through a small reception area that was meagerly furnished with a desk, chair and a pitiful, floor size plant that was in need of pruning and water. Then we entered a huge office. I gathered it took up the entire top floor of the building because it had a panoramic shape with windows that provided views from two angles. It was dark. Not because there weren't opportunities for light, but because the blinds, like hooded eyes, were barely open, and the wood was that dark knotty pine that could be found in the older buildings and houses in this part of Phoenix. Although large, the room was divided by a glass beaded curtain that made it appear much smaller then it was. Hanging beads? I didn't even know they still made those.

"Please have a seat." He motioned to one of two club chairs on the side opposite from the chair he slipped into behind the desk.

I took in the massive wooden book shelves that ran from the floor to the ceiling in almost every corner of the room. It looked more like a library than an office. Nearly every nook and cranny of the space was filled with books. There were hundreds of them. I wondered if he'd read them all.

Powers' huge desk was completely clean, except for two five by seven framed pictures that I could see held pictures of women; one with two boys and the other in a graduation cap and gown. The only other things on the desk were a telephone, laptop computer, a pen and a legal pad. "Your family," I asked pointing at the picture of the woman with the children.

He picked up the frame. "Yes, my baby sister and my nephews. They live in Nashville. Moved about two years ago when her husband was relocated with his company. I miss them terribly." He put the picture down, chuckled and reached for the other frame, "And this is my older sister. She's a workaholic attorney. I don't miss her as much."

"Local?" I asked, making small talk. I was so nervous, I was twisting the strap of my handbag around my fingers.

Powers noticed my fidgeting and sat back in his seat. "Los Angeles," he replied.

I nodded and attempted to smile. When I couldn't manage one, I slid my eyes away from his and surveyed the rest of the office space.

"So tell me, Ms. Watson." His voice was deep and strong, but still somehow gentle. It was time to get to business. "What can I do to help you today?"

I pulled my eyes away from the side of the room beyond the bead menagerie; the side where a sofa, television and small kitchenette were in residence. I wondered if Powers lived behind the glass veil.

"My husband is missing." I cleared my throat. "And so is a hundred and eighty thousand dollars of money that belonged to our non-profit organization."

Powers didn't blink. He merely nodded his head, picked up a pen and began to take notes. "Tell me more."

"What exactly do you need to know?" I clutched my purse to my abdomen. I was about to embarrass myself with my ridiculous tale. I didn't want to tell any of it that I didn't have to.

"Everything," Powers said. "Tell me how you met him and move forward. Don't leave anything out." He smiled and even though I hated to share my story, I couldn't help but relax as I recounted my first meeting with Leon. I remembered it like it was yesterday.

"Miss Taylor, what a pleasure to finally put a face to the voice." Leon Watson of Temple Realty stuck out one hand for a quick shake and put the other on my shoulder. "Please have a seat."

He was a tall, well made piece of eye candy; white teeth, nice haircut, and good diction. I was in instant like. He'd offered me a beverage and then immediately went into telling me how excited he was to list my property. I'd been thrilled, because no one else had been that enthusiastic about the neighborhood my grandmother's house was in.

"I'd like to sell it as is," I'd said. "The house is paid for. It was willed to me."

Leon shook his head. Explained that he thought that was fine, but if I was willing to invest seven or eight thousand dollars in it, that I could easily recoup that and another ten. He'd convinced me to take out a second mortgage on my house to pay for the renovations, helped me find inexpensive labor and even assisted me with painting the rooms. Of course by then we were no longer Miss Taylor and Mr. Watson. We were dating. Hot and heavy and I was falling in love with the man who told me it had always been his desire to work with the disadvantaged youth on Phoenix's south side. The Micah Center was his dream too.

"So, he told you he had a small amount of money saved. Continued to woo you until the house sold and then asked you to marry him." Powers matter-of-fact tone pulled me from my memory.

I took a deep breath, looked down at my hands and then back up at him. "That easy to figure out?"

Powers shook his head. "For me, but I'm a professional. This is what I do all day. Every day," he replied. "Except on Sundays." He smiled again and I wondered what he did on Sundays. I wondered if he was a Christian. I'd noticed he had a large plaque on the wall behind him with a scripture embossed on it. Scriptures didn't always mean people loved Jesus, but it was a sign that maybe I was dealing with someone with integrity. I wasn't trying to get robbed again.

"This happens all the time. It's very common," Powers voice interrupted my thoughts. "I had a similar case just a few months ago." I know he was trying to make me feel better about my foolishness, but it wasn't working. I should have thought through things more carefully. Leon really was too good to be true.

"If my instincts are correct you may be the victim of a Sweetheart Swindle." Powers put his pen down and sat back in his chair. "Most of us aren't aware of the vast amounts of information we give to others when we're chatting with them. In the workplace, at the gym, on a plane, but especially in a new business relationship such as one where you're listing a home. If, in fact, you've been a victim of a con artist, men like your husband, absorb every tidbit of information that you tell them. They observe things that other people don't notice. How we dress, our choice of hairstyles, the type of car we drive, what part of town we live, and a host of other clues are given away without us ever uttering a word. After a con artist gets his prey to start talking, the game begins. They'll do and say whatever they believe the victim wants to see and hear to get close to their money."

"But I don't get it, con artist prey on people with money. I barely had two dimes to rub together when Leon and I met." *Kind of like now*, I wanted to add.

"You had property and a dream. A dream that was going to require you to turn that property into cash. You shared that dream with him in your first meeting, so he knew you weren't going to close on one house and immediately buy another. He knew the money would be sitting around in an account until you spent it down."

I shook my head. I couldn't believe that I was some type of mark from the moment Leon met me. "Isn't it possible that he met a woman and ran off with her? I almost think that would make me feel better than being completely set up."

"It's possible." Powers picked up his pen. "But not likely. I mean, you've only been married four and a half months, Mrs. Watson. You're a very attractive woman.

You could easily hold his attention for longer than that. I can't imagine that he would be looking for a girlfriend so early in your marriage."

*Very attractive.* Those words were a shot of espresso. Boy did I need that hit, especially since I'd been thinking in addition to his being an obvious thief, that Leon's leaving had something to do with me; my inadequacies, the ones that crept to the forefront every time I met a man and every time one left me.

"Let me have his social security number and I'll do a background check." Powers picked up his pen again. "Hopefully, the one you have is his real one. We'll see what I find."

"So, you'll take my case?" My head bobbed like it was on springs. I didn't want to go through the humiliation of telling this story to another P.I. Besides he was a brother. I felt comfortable with him.

"I can." Powers said. "I have time and I think it'll be fairly easy to help you, especially if you have the right social. But even if you don't, we'll nail down who he is."

I nodded. "We need to talk about money." I gripped my purse tighter. "My husband has most of it. All I have is a credit card and there's not a whole lot of money on it."

"We can start with a retainer. I'll try to work quickly," he said as if it didn't matter how much money I had. "Just so you know the steps, I'll begin with a background check and put together a profile. I'll see if he's using any credit cards anywhere, using his I.D. for flights or trains, see if he's purchased a car. If I can't find him actively moving, I'll try to locate him based on something from his past."

I was overwhelmed. I couldn't believe I was sitting here talking about background checks and profiles. I was supposed to be at work groaning about my accounts and my boss. Dreaming about the day I could sit in an office, side by side with my husband running our center, not sitting in a private investigators office. My eyes began to get wet. I fought letting the tears fall. "That sounds expensive."

"It doesn't have to be," he replied. "Trust me, I'm fast."

I nodded. Instinctively, I trusted Powers, which wasn't really saying much, because I'd instinctively trusted Leon. But I was here. I had to try something. I reached into my purse for my credit card. "Let's get started."

# seven

My days were starting to run into each other. I hadn't left the house since I'd met with Powers. I had even let myself run out of ice-cream. Erin would not stop harassing me. She was my best friend, but I was starting to wonder if she had a multiple personality disorder. Her messages were getting on my last nerve. "Girl, I told you he wasn't no good" and "I'm so sorry this happened to you. We should pray." She was making me crazier than I was making myself. And then there was Kym, my virtual administrative assistant for the Micah Foundation. We hadn't talked since Friday morning. She'd been calling and texting and sending emails non-stop.

"Tamera." Kym barked my name and pulled me out of the fog. "Are you listening to me? I need to get the invitations out to the corporate donors, but you haven't approved the verbiage, yet."

*I should tell her,* I thought. She was invested in this project too. Even though she was being paid, Kym had always gone above and beyond the dollars she invoiced me for, because she believed in what Leon and I were doing. *I should tell her.* But I couldn't. I just couldn't say it today. I washed my hands over my face and bit my lip.

"Tam, is something wrong?"

I forgot we were on a video conference call. I looked at my computer monitor and found Kym staring back at me. "I just need coffee," I said. "It's six a.m."

"And that's not new. We always meet at six a.m." Kym's irritation was rising. "Tamera, you've been acting strange for days. Not showing up for our meetings and I haven't even seen Leon. What's going on? Is there something I need to know?"

I grimaced. "I just need a little more time. Some things are happening with the 501C." I felt guilty about lying to her. I was lying to everyone these days.

"What things?" Kym asked. "You don't even need that to open. It's not a priority item right now."

I didn't want Kym to see my face, so I reached down into a drawer like I was looking for something as I spoke. "I should have it resolved in a day or so. The lawyer is helping. Really it's minor." I sat back up to face her.

Kym held up a legal pad that was filled with items. "Then we need to get through this list."

I nodded and Kym proceeded to tell me the fifty things I needed to do in the next week to keep us on schedule for the opening. I pretended to be listening, said "Okay, alright, sure and uh-hum." I nodded as appropriate. I even faked taking notes.

"I'll email it all to you again." There was a little less irritation in her voice. "I really need you to at least approve the invitation, and the artwork today. Oh and the furniture. If you want chairs for people to sit in you have to pick them today. The supplier has a three week delivery window."

"I hear you, Kym. I'll do all those things today."

"Make sure you do." Kym wagged a finger at me. "We'll reconvene this time tomorrow."

"Yes," I said. "I have to get dressed for work." She nodded and I pushed the mouse to end the call.

Maybe I could send her an email. People broke up by text message these days. An email wouldn't be too bad. I needed to get her off the payroll after all. I didn't have money to pay her to keep working for a center that wasn't going to happen. I sighed and turned off the computer. After I left the office, I slowly marched up the stairs to my bedroom and climbed back under the covers on my side. Leon's side continued to be undisturbed. I dared not stretch my body across the expanse of mattress. Doing so would be a reminder of the awful place I was in right now. *A reminder like that closet*, I thought, looking at the now closed door where Leon's possessions remained. The closet full of his clothes and shoes he apparently didn't need any more now that he was living it up with my money.

My heart was so heavy I thought I'd die. I reached for my Bible on the nightstand and opened it to the marker I'd placed in Deuteronomy chapter thirty-two. I had been reading it before I fell asleep last night.

> *"For the LORD will vindicate His people, And will have compassion on His servants, When He sees that their strength is gone, And there is none remaining, bond or free."*

*The Lord will vindicate His people.* I'd chosen that passage of scripture, because it was the one hanging in Powers' office. I thought it an odd choice for décor, even the office of a P.I., but then I considered I'd been in a room where glass beads hung in a solid panel between spaces. Not that there was any bad Bible, but Powers' taste was probably in his mouth.

*When He sees that their strength is gone.* I read it again and thought about my situation. I needed God to vindicate me. I could only hope the scripture applied to sweetheart scams, because my strength was definitely gone. I closed the Bible, stared at the ceiling and said a prayer. "Lord, please help me. I'm in so much trouble. All I wanted was to love my husband. Start a family and do some good for the community. How could things have come to this?"

God was silent. Hope did not engulf me. The answer to my problems did not fall from the sky. Even if I tried, I was hard pressed to remove the layer of self-pity that was caked on my body from head to toe. My cell phone vibrated. I reached for it and opened the pending text message. It was from my graphic artist. I sighed and read:

{Hope to catch you before you start work. I really need you to approve the artwork for the posters and postcards or the price is going to go up for printing.}

And so it began, phone calls from everyone. The caterer wanted to finalize the menu, the videographer and photographers were looking for their deposits, the event planner had details to discuss including her fee. Everyone wanted money from me. Money I couldn't pay. The only thing that I owned was renovations on a building the city gave to me. We were going to lease the furniture. Leon's idea of course. I didn't quite agree with him on that, but now I understood. Greedy dog wanted all the cash for himself.

"God help me. What am I going to do?" I sat at my desk. Looked at all the emails and invoices that were waiting for me and began to pray into between sobs. I had called in sick for the third day in a row and now I really was sick. I climbed the stairs again, looked at the door to Leon's closet. I should just clean it out. Take all his stuff out and burn it at a dump. But I didn't have the energy to do anything. After the barrage of responsibility that had fallen on me this morning, I just couldn't do anything about his stuff.

"How dare you leave this mess behind for me to clean up!" I yelled at the door. More tears fell. I crawled into bed and tried to fall asleep, but I could not stop thinking about men—all the men in my life who had wronged me, starting with my father. He'd walked out on our family when I was six. Every boyfriend I'd ever had cheated on me, my brother got himself in trouble and was in jail and now my husband. I was a magnet for disaster with the opposite sex, a complete failure. I cried some more. Eventually the sobbing gave way to a heaviness that lulled me into sleep.

# eight

I heard it in my dreams. The phone rang again and it would not stop. House phone, cell phone, ring...ring...ring...I finally answered it. I hadn't even taken the time to look at the caller I.D. My voice was so weak and my greeting so pitiful that my boss would have been convinced I was at death's door if it was her.

"Ms. Watson, I've been trying to reach you all afternoon. I have a report." Kemuel Powers' voice came through the earpiece and miraculously bathed me in warmth. The man had a power, really a super-power that made me feel like he could save me from this horrible mess. I sat up in the bed. "That was fast." I'd just met with him yesterday.

"I work fast." For a fleeting second I imagined that crooked smile I'd seen fall across his face when he'd attempted to make me laugh; about what I couldn't even remember now, but I remembered the smile. It was incredibly handsome. Just like old Hill Harper himself. "Look, I'm on my way out of the office. Wednesday's are my early day, Bible study and all, but if you don't mind, I can stop by your house and share it with you. You're on my way home."

So he didn't live behind the beaded veil. That was good news. I nodded as if he could see me and cleared my throat. "Of course," I said. "Please, I would appreciate it."

Forty minutes and a quick shower later, I was letting Powers into my house. I showed him into the family room which I managed to clean up just before he rang the bell. The trash was now jammed with ice-cream cartons and pizza boxes and potato chips bags. I was pathetic and I could tell I'd gained at least five pounds, because my all my jeans were too tight.

I watched as Powers glided across the room and took a seat. I was reminded by his presence that I no longer had a man and although I was nowhere near in the market to find a new one, the eating had to stop or I'd be as big as a house by the time I wanted to date.

"Leon Watson is at Roman's Palace," Powers said as soon as my rear hit the cushion on the sofa beside him.

"Roman's Palace?" I questioned with my tone.

"Las Vegas." Powers handed me a file folder stapled with a typed report. I glanced at it, flipped the page. There were pictures. "He's been there since he left Phoenix."

I was staring at a picture of my thieving husband at a card table. Grinning from ear to ear. Some cheap woman standing behind him. "You went to Vegas?"

"No, I have a detective buddy there who I pay a fee to follow up and get pictures. It helps cut down on expenses for my clients and travel for me."

I continued to flip through the pictures. Roman's Palace was clearly a five star hotel. Gaudy, but posh. There were pictures of him by the pool, in a restaurant, in a jewelry store putting a necklace around the woman's neck. I looked down at the meager diamond on my finger, the one I was still wearing, still holding out hope that this was all a bad dream. I put the report on the sofa, stood and slid the ring off my finger and shoved it in the pocket of my jeans. "So, he's definitely not kidnapped or dead." I whispered those words to myself and then turned to Powers. "I guess you were wrong about the other woman though."

"Unfortunately, I wasn't." Powers paused and I knew he was about to say something really foul. "The woman is someone he's known for a long time. Leon has a record. He's served time for theft by deception, theft by taking – both are fraud charges. He's a con man. A real professional. He's done this exact same thing before two years ago in Houston. Stole the proceeds of the sale of a house from his fiancé. He just upped the ante with the corporate funds."

I was still stuck on the *unfortunately I wasn't* part. He'd conveniently avoided explaining that and although I was disgusted about Leon, I was confused about where Powers was going. "What does that have to do with the woman in the pictures?"

Powers pursed his lips for a few seconds. "Her name is Delilah Owens. She's got a rap sheet too. That's how I found him. The room is registered in one of her aliases. They've been busted together before. They went to the same high school. Graduated the same year."

My stomach flipped and my hand flew over my mouth. I was going to be sick. I was going to vomit three days worth of pizza, Chinese food and ice-cream. Tears filled my eyes; anger burned the inside of my nostrils. I felt the room spin and then Powers powerful hands gripped my arm and back. "Have a seat." His breath whisked past my ear. Like a spell it instantly quelled the nausea. "I know this is a shock."

I sat and burst into tears. Powers joined me on the sofa again. He must have reached across the table for tissues, because he handed me a fistful. Tissues, they were everywhere in this room. I'd purchased five boxes the other day because I couldn't stop crying. I peeked out of the corner of my eye at Powers. He looked so uncomfortable. He was probably used to delivering this horrible news from across a desk in his office, but now he had a weeping woman next to him. I stood and walked across the room to the window where I could blow my nose without ruining his poor ear drum. I pulled myself together and stopped the waterworks, which was easy to do, because another emotion was taking over.

Leon was a professional con artist and he'd known that hooker in the pictures since high school. Steam was rising in my belly. Anger was boiling in my blood. He'd married me. Laid in the bed with me every night; made love to me, learned all my fears and my secrets, so he could con me out of my grandmother's inheritance. Oh heck no. The crying was stopping right now. "That bastard."

"Ms. Watson, I think it's time for you to consult an attorney."

"Tamera," I said. "Please call me Tamera, and I already have." I turned back to look at him. He was standing also.

"Talked to an attorney. She didn't have anything to say that I wanted to hear."

"You can press charges. I think the evidence that he's got a track record of this will prove you've been a victim."

I took a few steps, closed the space between us. "I don't want to be a victim," I said. "Do you know of any way I can get money back, and I'm not talking the way an attorney would advise me?"

"Something an attorney wouldn't advise you to do?" Powers frowned, but I could tell he knew what I meant.

"I know it's wrong," I said. "I know I shouldn't be trying to take matters into my own hands, but I have to try something. My mother and grandmother raised a fighter. I'm not this woman who lies down and gets trampled on. I fight back."

"I'm not judging you." Powers swallowed noticeably. "It's just things like this sometimes get out of hand and I don't want to see you get hurt anymore than you've been hurt."

I didn't respond. Powers stood. Our eyes met for a moment and he seemed to be assessing me. "I know I sound unstable, but I'm not. I am acting in faith here. I trust God to take care of me. To vindicate me and make this right."

Powers nodded. I sensed he was thinking about the scripture in his office.

"Getting the money back is the way to make it right," I said. "So, please tell me what to do."

Powers sighed like he knew I was going to ask him this difficult question. He answered like he'd already thought about the answer. "I'd have to know where he was keeping it first and then there's the matter of getting him to hand it over. He's not likely to do that willingly."

I shook my head. "I'm not concerned about him being willing. You find the money. Can you do that? I have about a thousand dollars left and I get paid on next Wednesday. That's another thirteen hundred if I don't eat." I attempted a smile. "If you find the money I'll take care of the rest."

Powers looked mystified. "How are you going to do that?"

"I'm still his wife. The same way he was able to take all as my husband, I can take all as his widow."

"Widow?" Powers eyebrows knit together.

"Yes, widow, because after I get my hands on my money, I'm going to kill that low life thief."

# nine

After Powers delivered the bad news about Leon, I'd watched a few more episodes of *Snapped* and realized if I was going to kill Leon, I had to have a gun. I shifted on the sofa and like the Princess and the Pea, I'd felt my wedding rings in my pocket under me. Leon had paid twelve hundred dollars for the rings, so I knew I should be able to pawn them for at least half. Boy, was I in for a rude awakening.

"I'll give you four-fifty," Big Al of Big Al's Pawn and Loan scratched his belly as he examined my diamond through an eye lens.

"Four-fifty," I protested.

"Lady, this is barely a carat. I got rings coming out of my ears in here. Four-fifty is it."

I looked over Al's shoulder at the gun case. "I want one of those." I nodded. "Will four-fifty do it?"

Al laughed as he pulled a set of keys from his pants pocket and opened the case. "Live in a bad neighborhood?"

I smirked behind his back. He removed a gun from the very back of the cabinet. "Smith and Wesson double action .45," he said. "Lightweight. Perfect gun for a lady and that price is a steal."

He put it in my hand. It didn't feel that light. It felt like trouble. "Does it work for sure?"

"I don't sell stuff that don't work, lady. You need to take some lessons on how to use it so you don't kill yourself. Shooter's Galaxy has classes."

"What about bullets?" I asked putting it on the counter.

"You have to get your own ammo. You can get 'em anywhere." He reached back in the cabinet and pulled out a silver case about the size of a net book computer. He opened it, removed a small cylinder and dropped it in my hand.

"What's this?"

"A silencer. Muffles the sound of the bullet. Came with the gun. Both these and the case are yours for the low asking price of four hundred and fifty dollars."

Big Al smiled and I owned a gun.

# ten

Bang! Bang! Bang!

"Pull your shoulders back and straighten out this elbow." Bruce, my shooting instructor helped position my arms. I squinted to improve my view of the black and white bull's eye target down the range and fired off another round. I was getting used to having this hard, black metal in my hands. At first it felt like a bug, like something that crawled up my arm that I needed to shake off. But now, almost four hours into my second session of "Basic Shooting" lesson, it was feeling like an extension of my hand.

"You sure this is your first gun? You're pretty good." Bruce winked at me.

I smiled and shifted my feet to adjust my weight. "My first time," I replied. "I think I like it."

"Most women do. It's the power. You chicks dig it." Bruce laughed and I tried not to be insulted that a kid in his early twenties had just called me a chick.

"After this, you've got one more round." He moved on to another student. I was glad to see him go. I didn't need him anymore. I had this hitting the mark stuff down to a tee. I had gotten used to the recoil when I fired. I had gotten used to noise. I had gotten used to the idea of firing a gun period. I inserted a new clip of blank bullets and pushed the start button. My target flipped down and up popped the last round Bruce had told me about. The one with figures of men and women moving; targets that challenged me to shift and move and shoot. I imagined Leon and his skank girlfriend, Delilah and pulled back on the trigger.

Bang! Bang! Bang!

I blocked out the voice in my head that said, "Vengeance is mine", because I had a piece of revenge right in my hand. One that was sure to get me results here and now, not in five or ten years or in the after-life. My targets were on the move again.

Bang! Bang! Bang!

My bullet clip was empty. I removed my protective eye and ear gear. The paper bodies down the lane were full of holes in all the right places. I smiled. Both of those no good Negroes were dead.


I pulled into my driveway and noted a car rolling in right behind me. Erin. I'd been lucky she'd had to go to Denver last week for a training conference, but now she was back and I was about to get an earful. I opened my car door and grabbed my bags.

"Are you out of your mind?" Erin yanked my poor Honda's door back like she was trying to pull it off the hinges. "Do you know how many times I've called you?"

How could I not know? She'd called me almost as many times as I'd called Leon when he first got missing. I stayed calm, hoping it would diffuse her temper. "I left you a message."

She stepped back to give me room to climb out. "Girl, you don't leave me no message on my voice mail. I've been worried sick about you and the whole Leon the Loser situation. I can't believe you didn't take my calls."

I pushed the key fob to lock my car and turned to walk to the house. She was right behind me. "Erin, I know you like to be kept up to date, but really, I've been pretty busy cleaning up the mess Leon the Loser, as you so eloquently put it, left behind."

Erin grabbed my arm and stopped me in my tracks. "It ain't about being kept up to date. You're my best friend. I'm worried about you." She released my arm. "How could you be so insensitive, Tam?"

"I know, I'm sorry." I avoided meeting her eyes.

"And I'm told you haven't been to the office all week."

"I went to the doctor on Friday. I have a note. I'm out with the flu." We entered the house. I dropped my bag on the kitchen table and pulled the oversized tee-shirt I'd been wearing over my head. Erin was still on my heels like a little poodle that wasn't getting their owner's attention.

"You need to get your butt back to work. I know you were planning to quit eventually, but *surely* now you need it." Surely had lots of emphasis on it. Erin's eyes swept my body. "And where are you coming from looking like one of Charlie's Angels?"

I looked down at my all black spandex outfit and sneakers. I did look like a Ninja, but I sure wasn't going to tell her I'd been at Shooter's Galaxy. She'd really think I'd lost it. "I was working out." That much was true. My arms were killing me. "The doctor's note will have me covered. I have more than enough sick time."

Erin's fist went to her hips. "Working out. Since when do you work out?"

"Since I have about five hundred percent more stress." I opened the refrigerator and pulled out a bottle of water. "Would you like one?"

Erin looked at her watch. "No, girl. I have to go. I've got to get my hair tightened and then I have a voice lesson." She reached up and scratched her head. The entire monstrosity of a weave moved with her fingers.

I walked closer to Erin and hugged her. "I'm sorry. I should have talked to you. I've just been in a funk. I needed some time to get my head together. I'm feeling much better."

"Yeah, you're looking pretty good for somebody's that's been beat out of one eighty." She pulled her purse higher on her shoulder. "Did you talk to a lawyer?"

"I did. Not much I can do." I turned her in the direction of the door. "I'll tell you all about it later. Go get your wig done, nothing worse than a loose weave in the choir stand."

Erin pulled the front door open and stepped through. "I'm going to ring you after my lesson. Don't ignore my call heifer."

"I won't."

"And don't forget I'm singing a solo tomorrow, so I expect you to be in church."

"I will."

"And wear something a little clingy." She sized up my attire again. "Who knew you looked like J. Lo under those old ladies suits."

I smirked. Erin walked out and I let my body fall against the door. Church. No way. I was not doing well with people. I felt like everyone could look at me and tell what a fool I was. I had a scarlet letter made out of a big fat "F" on my forehead. People would be asking me about the opening and I just – couldn't. I couldn't tell them the entire thing was off. The whispering would begin and the rumors would start flying. I wasn't going back to church yet. Not until I got the money and re-strategized. I needed to hear from Powers.

I walked into the kitchen and lifted my handbag off of the gun case. I opened it and took out the sleek weapon. I'd done good today. Maybe I should have been a cop. Guns were fun.

*Vengeance is mine.* There was that voice in my head again, making me second guess myself, and filling my soul with guilt. "I don't want vengeance, Lord. I just want my money." I know God wasn't exactly trying to hear that crap from me, but I had to get the money back and I didn't expect some angel to drop out of the sky and hand it to me, not after the way I'd so foolishly let my husband have it. Before God could say something else, the doorbell rang. *Erin.* What did she forget? I put the gun back in the case and looked around. Erin hadn't had anything but her purse and it was on her shoulder when she walked out, so that meant she had something else to say. I pulled the door open. My breath caught in my throat. It wasn't Erin.

# eleven

"Not a great way to open your door." I moved aside and Kemuel Powers stepped in. "Lot of home invasions in Phoenix and most happen in the daytime."

I shook my head. "My best friend just pulled out and I assumed it was her."

"And that's something people scouting for a home to break into look for – recent visitors leaving. They know you'll think the doorbell is the person returning."

Sufficiently chastised, I nodded. I gushed inside though. Something about a man lecturing me was sexy. Reminded me of Leon, minus the new bull's-eye I'd permanently etched on his forehead.

"Sorry, I slipped into cop mode." He flashed me that crooked smile I'd come to love seeing. "Ten years on Phoenix P.D."

"I should have guessed you'd been a cop. Isn't that where most P.I.'s come from, the police force?"

"Yeah, I'd say about seventy percent of us do."

A moment passed between us when neither of us said anything. I noticed his eyes traveled the length of my spandex clad body. I was wishing I still had on my tee-shirt, because suddenly I was feeling exposed. He could see every curve of my "twenty pounds overweight" body. I broke the silence. "Did you have an update for me?"

Powers was startled out of his daze. He reached into his jacket pocket. "I'm sorry. Of course. That's why I'm here. I forgot to charge my cell phone, so I thought I'd just take a chance—"

"It's okay." I shook my head. "I appreciate the personal service." He was staring again. "Let me just go change."

"No." The word came out of his mouth like a rocket. I raised an eyebrow. "You're fine." His eyes fell to my hips. "Really fine—and I won't be long at all."

I swayed an open hand in the direction of the family room. "Let's sit."

He looked past me into the kitchen. "Actually, if you don't mind, someplace where there's a table." I remembered how uncomfortable he seemed on the sofa next to me. His long legs didn't have any place to go and then there was the crying. I could see how the space might have seemed intimate. He probably thought I was going to freak out again.

"The kitchen." I turned, and he followed. I was self-conscious about the fact that my spandex wearing Beyonce-wanna-be bootie was bouncing in front of him. I was glad it was a short walk. We entered my kitchen and as we did I saw the gun case. Powers would know exactly what it was and being a crackerjack detective, he wouldn't miss it. I tried to put my body in between it and him. As he was taking a seat I shoved it back under my handbag. Too late. I could tell by the frown on his face that he'd seen it. "It's a precaution," I said.

Powers reached for his tie knot and loosened it slightly. I wondered where he was coming from in a shirt and tie. "I know I may sound like the poster boy for an anti-NRA campaign, but guns are dangerous."

"I took lessons." I crossed my arms in front of me.

Powers frowned. "That doesn't make them any less dangerous."

"I'm a good shot for a newbie. Even my instructor said so." I pulled the refrigerator open and removed two bottles of water. I placed one in front of Powers and slipped into the chair across from him.

Powers stared me down, and I added, "Being conned has left me feeling, I don't know – exposed. Having the gun has helped my confidence."

He shook his head. "A gun is not the place to find confidence."

I took a long sip of my water. I was stalling. The confidence thing had been a lie and I sensed he knew it. "I have to fix this situation. I need to confront Leon, if for nothing else than to look him in the face after what he did to me. He made a fool of me."

"You're not a fool." He was quick with his words. Our eyes connected and then he looked away."

"Oh, no? Tell me what you see when you look at me or any other woman who's been shanked out of her life savings so easily."

"Not a fool." He shook his head. "You're being too hard on yourself. I'm telling you, I do this for a living. I know a silly woman when I meet one. When I look at you, I see someone who's strong. You haven't fallen in a bottle or tried drugs. You're not lying in bed sleeping it away or worse. You're standing, thinking and planning. Heck, you hired me." He smiled. "I'm impressed."

"But..."

"No buts. Let me tell you what I know." He reached into his jacket and pulled out a typewritten report. "I followed your husband for three days. I hate to tell you this, but he's spending money like a fool. Gambling, eating high, letting the woman shop. He'll be broke inside of a few months if we don't get it back."

I noticed Powers said "we", which felt good. I'd been feeling so alone in this, but it still didn't take the sting out of Leon letting the woman shop when he'd been so cheap with me. "We're saving for our future." How many times had he told me that?

Powers continued. "I followed him to a bank. He doesn't have an account, just a bank deposit box. I have source trying to find out if it's in his name."

"How do you know he doesn't have an account?" I asked.

"I'm having a source check, but my guess is no account. He's stupid, but not that stupid. You could find a bank account. Boxes aren't as easy to find. Plus when he went in the bank, the clerk escorted him straight to boxes."

I nodded. This was progress. At least we knew where the money was. "What if it's in her name?"

Powers raised an eyebrow and I got question and statement in the furrow. "Yeah, I know. He's stupid, but not that stupid," I said.

"Not hardly," Powers added.

"Well." I stood and put my hands on my hips. "I guess I'm going to Vegas."

"That's not necessary. I'll be going back. I hope to hear about the bank account on Monday. I'm trying to find out if it's in one of his aliases."

I shook my head. "I can't afford to pay you anymore."

"Don't worry about the money. Let's call your attorney on Monday. We can have her file an order to seize the box."

"The box that we don't know whose name it's in? And as for the bank account, Leon could have another identity by now. Don't you think it's likely he would with all the alias names you had in the background report?"

Powers skepticism was all over his face. "It's likely. But Mrs. Watson, you can't just show up and expect to there not to be an altercation."

I lifted a brow. "I'm not Mrs. Watson. I never was." It hurt to say the words. "I was someone he met and took advantage of."

Powers shook his head. "I'm just trying to remember what I'm doing here." Once again our eyes locked. He cleared his throat. "I mean, I'm trying to stick to a strategic plan. That's what P.I.'s do. We plan."

I nodded understanding, but I heard what he said. Trying to remember what he was doing here. My heart was thudding.

"Mrs.— Wa—"

"Please, call me Tamera." My voice was husky.

"Tamera, I can't in good conscious let you go deal with this by yourself. Plus I mean, you used the word widow last week and now you have a gun."

If I hadn't noticed he was looking past me at my bags on the counter, I would have lingered on the fact that he'd actually said my name. It was the first time and coming off his tongue it sounded liked it was spun in silk.

I shook my head. "Forget I said widow, because if something should happen to the scum, something like a bullet in his head, then I would have said I was going to kill him and you'll be a witness."

Powers stood and took the few steps necessary to the counter. He pulled the gun case from under the bag and opened it. "I got it from a pawn shop. I actually inherited a rifle from my grandfather, or grandmother. It was hers after my grandfather died, but it's too big to lug around."

Power nodded. "Do you think your grandparents would want to see you in prison?" I looked down at my sneakers. Thought about my brother. "I've watched people, a lot of them women, go to prison everyday over a man and some money, or a man and some woman. It happens, Tamera. Don't do this."

Tears were threatening to break. Powers hands were on my forearms. "If you have to go to Vegas, let me go with you."

I wanted to fall into this man's arms. I was under his superpower for real. I was broke, scared, angry as all get up and at this moment very vulnerable to his touch. Leon and I made love everyday. I missed it. Now I knew how and why women slept with their lawyers and therapist. The need for affection was dancing on every nerve ending in my body. *Lord help me*, I thought. I moved out of his grasp.

"I have to preach tomorrow evening's service. But I promise, we can leave first thing Monday morning."

"Did you say preach? You're a preacher?"

"Evangelist. I'm still in ministry school. I deliver the evening message on the last Sunday of the month."

"A preaching private detective?"

"Yep." He put his hands in his pants pockets and rocked back on his heels.

"How do you do this work and then minister the word?"

"I think this work really helps with the ministry. I mean other than a street ministry, where do you see and get closer to the problems, fragility and fears that we have?" I thought about all that Powers had witnessed in my life and realized he was right. He'd seen me at the lowest moment in my life. There wasn't much worse than betrayal. "Will you wait for me?" He almost sounded like he was begging. Those lush brown eyes looked like they were. I nodded yes. My angel had dropped from the sky.

# twelve

I reconsidered. I didn't want to involve Powers in this mess. Especially now that I knew he was Minister Powers. Not that I really planned to kill Leon or that garden tool he was laid up with, but I wasn't above shooting a brother in the toe to get my money back. I'd seen Leon's toes. The man was fine, but those toes were not. That raggedy pinky toe definitely wasn't worth that much, so if a sistah had to fire off a round...well, so be it.

I thought about calling my thug cousin Dre and asking him to come with me, but with Dre came drama. Four times in the county lockup and one three year stint upstate. Dre was a career criminal with a hot temper. I'd end up in a shoot out with the Vegas police department, the SWAT team and Homeland Security messin' with that Negro. At a minimum we'd go to prison, but more than likely, we'd be killed.

Powers wanted me to do things the legal way. Wait on the bank, get a lawyer, when I knew the only way to deal with my low-life husband was face to face with the barrel of the .45 pointing at his chest. That was the way to get the money out of the box.

The phone rang and it was Erin. Her voice lesson was over. "Fill me in, girl," she said and I told her everything. Except the part about Shooter's Galaxy.

"Dang, Tam. I was just kidding when I said he was a crook. I mean. He's a crook for real. I mean that mess is just crazy. You could have been hurt or killed. People like that will stop at nothing to get what they want."

Finally, some sympathy from my unsympathetic friend. "It's pretty deep."

"So what's up next? I mean, what you gonna do? Try to press charges or something?"

"Powers is checking on some things. We'll figure out a plan after that."

"Powers, that's a nice name for a detective."

"It's Kemuel Powers."

"Sounds like a brother. I keep hearing the word 'we'. Is he single?"

I thought about Powers and wanted to tell her how absolutely yummy he was. How tall and handsome and smart he was, his nice full lips and...

"Tam, is he single or what?"

She'd messed up my fantasy. "Girl, I don't know. I think so. He doesn't wear a ring, but then again, half the time neither did Leon."

"Well, you find out for a sistah. I might need to hire him to check a background or two out for me."

"What's that got to do with him being single?"

"Honey, you know those cop and detective types like a damsel in distress. All I gotta do is turn on the tears and if a background check come back bad, I can slide Powers in as a pinch hitter." Erin laughed at her own joke. She was getting on my last nerve.

"I'ma go. *Snapped* is about to start and I don't like to miss the beginning."

"You need to stop watching all that craziness and get out of that house," Erin replied. "Come go to the singles service with me tonight."

*Singles service.* Was she out of her mind? "Good night Erin." I hung up the phone.

It really was time for *Snapped*. The episode was about a murdering con artist. Great, the one thing I didn't want to see. But I watched it and turned off the television when it was done with a new knowledge. Con artists never stay anywhere for long. I had already decided that I was going to Vegas alone, but this new information confirmed, I didn't have time to wait for Powers. Leon and Delilah had been in Vegas for over a week. They most assuredly would be leaving soon.

I picked up the phone and called Roman's Palace, asked for Desiree Holmes, the alias Delilah was using. "Please hold for Ms. Holmes," the attendant said. I hung up before it connected because I'd found out what I wanted to know. They were still there.

I jumped up and ran up the stairs. I had to get to Vegas before they picked up and moved, before they decided to go to the Caribbean or Europe. I threw some clothes and toiletries in a suitcase and pulled the small bag down the stairs. I put an empty duffel bag inside the suitcase, just in case I needed a bag for the money. I reached for the gun case and just as I was about to put it in the suitcase, I realized, I didn't have any bullets. I didn't even know where people got bullets from. I went into my office and opened my ever trusty phone book for ammunition sales. Phoenix was a gun toter's dreamland. They sold bullets everywhere, even in Wal-mart, so Wal-mart it was. I was completely out of cash until payday, but I still had my credit card. Powers hadn't billed me for anything beyond the initial retainer, so I could still access the available credit.

Getting bullets at Wal-mart was like buying anything else. I could have told the clerk I wanted soap, or a DVD player and he would have pushed the box across the counter the exact same way. I got back to the house and noticed the sun was going down. I hated driving at night, plus there was the added safety risk. I was already tired. I took a long hot soak in my tub, climbed into bed and set the alarm for five thirty a.m.

I was yawning and I wasn't even in the car yet. I hadn't been able to sleep last night. My nerves were on edge. I couldn't believe what my life had come to. Two weeks ago I was happily married and about to embark on the business venture of my dreams. Now I was alone, planning to shoot my husband in the pinky toe with a gun I'd purchased from Big Al's Pawn and Loan. Not to mention – broke. Flat broke. It didn't get much worse than this. Outside of an awful disease or a natural disaster, life did not shift like this in less than two weeks.

I poured coffee into my travel mug, grabbed the bagel and cream cheese sandwich I'd made, set the security system and piled into my car. I yawned again. Lord how I wish I could fly. I started the car. No point in dwelling on what I couldn't do. There was the matter of the gun and the fact that I couldn't afford a plane ticket.

I arrived in Vegas five hours later. The drive had been exhausting. I was so high on No Doze and bad gas station coffee that I was probably going to turn into a gaudy Vegas neon light as soon as the sun went down. I pulled into the parking lot of the hotel I'd reserved for the one night I anticipated needing one. It was an inexpensive spot that resembled the French Quarter so much that it saddened me. Leon and I had spent our honey moon in New Orleans. I'd known the hotel was named Orleans but I hadn't really made the connection until I pulled into the parking lot. I wanted to cry, but I woman-ed up.

It was just after noon and I realized leaving Phoenix so early had been a bad idea. I was exhausted, but couldn't check into my room until three o'clock. I didn't have the energy to confront anyone right now. I'd drop from sheer exhaustion. I decided to risk that they would let me check in early and thankfully the front desk clerk believed my glazed eyes were due to sleep deprivation and not a drug induced high. I'm sure the ten dollar tip I slid her didn't hurt either.

I sank into the mattress. It was unbelievably comfortable. It felt good to be in a bed that wasn't my own, because mine reminded me of my husband.

I had calls to make before I fell asleep. The first was to Roman's Palace. I asked for Desiree's room again. I didn't get an answer but I was satisfied that it was past checkout time and the lovebirds hadn't checked out. Then I sent a text to Erin's cell phone, advising her I was out of town for a couple days and would not be in church to hear her sing the big solo. I also told her not to worry. She'd be angry about both.

The last call was the office number for Powers. I told him I was in Vegas already, taking care of the business I needed to handle. I'd update him when I returned. I didn't want the man changing his schedule to accommodate a trip to Vegas that he didn't need to make. Then I curled up in the bed and fell into a deep sleep.

# thirteen

Several hours later I was standing in the lobby of the luxurious Roman's Palace. It was dripping with imagery and architecture steeped in the theme of Ancient Rome. Huge white statues of naked men, women and cherubs with bright gold headdresses were everywhere. I can't say that it would have been my choice of hotels to stay in, but this was clearly baller-land.

It was six p.m. and I didn't want to waste any time figuring the joint out so I paid a hotel maid to tell me which floor the Royal Suite was on and then threw more money at an elevator attendant to swipe a card that gave me access to the floor. I was greasing palms left and right. Who said you couldn't get an education watching television? I learned about tipping the help from *Lifetime* and *Snapped*.

I stood in the corridor outside of the Royal Suite and realized that there was no way for me to know whether or not Leon was actually inside. The place was sound proof. I swear I could hear my own heart beating. The quiet made me nervous, and even though it was freezing all over the hotel, I was starting to perspire. The overpriced hotdog I'd eaten was doing flips in my stomach and that wasn't making it any better.

*Why are you here?* The voice in my head was back. I tried to push it out, but I knew, this was not who I was. I was not some crazy person who had "snapped" and stood outside of suites in Las Vegas with a gun in my purse. I was a decent woman, a Christian who went to church every Sunday, was raised by women who taught me to pray and trust God. I was better than this. Tears began to burn my eyes. *Vengeance is mine,* the voice said. *"For the LORD will vindicate His people";* the scripture in Powers office was another reminder that God would repay. I'd made a mistake. My stomach churned again and knew I would actually be physically ill soon. I had to get out of here. I had to go back to Phoenix. I had to let Powers and an attorney make this right.

When the elevator made it to the lobby, I rushed through the door and found the closest ladies room and threw up. I threw up the hotdog, my pain, my frustration, my pride and my anger. When I was done, I sat in that stall for a long time. I thought about my choices. The choice to date Leon, marry him, start the business, co-mingle our funds. All of these were my choices and they had been bad ones, because as much as Erin got on my last nerve with her "I told you so's" she was right, I didn't really know him for more than a few months before I was running my behind down the aisle talking about "I do". I stood to weak feet and left the restroom. It was time to go home.

I returned to the lobby and was just about to ask one of the staff how to get back to the parking area when I saw them. Leon and a tall, bad weave wearing, skinny, cheap looking heifer in a shiny red, micro mini-dress were heading in the direction of the main casino. Leon didn't even look like the conservative man I had been married to for the last four months. He was wearing a red sequin smoking jacket. It looked like he'd put an S-curl or some other craziness in his hair. He had an earring in his right ear which held a huge diamond stud. He looked like a pimp and Delilah looked like a hooker. They turned a corner. I followed. I started thinking, there had to be three hundred people milling in the lobby area of this hotel, and I'd spotted them. This had to be fate. An angel had fallen from the sky. I was supposed to get my money back.

Leon and Delilah entered an area called Restaurant Row. There were people waiting in long lines in front of all the many different eateries in this area of the hotel. They walked hand in hand until they made it to what looked like the very last and notably the most exclusive restaurant of them all. At least forty couples were in line waiting, but apparently the gold VIP card Leon waived got them to the front of the line. No doubt some perk for being in one of those ridiculously expensive suites. Once they were inside, I squeezed in beyond the crowd to the front and watched them through the gold tinted window. I glanced down at a glass case that held the menu. I thought I would faint. They were going to spend at least two hundred and fifty dollars on dinner, easy. At least. If he'd been in Vegas since he left that was almost ten days in a seven hundred dollars a night suite, two hundred dollar meals, gambling and that heifer's shopping. He was probably almost into twenty-five grand by now and no telling what they were driving. I was sick, really sick. No,

I was not sick. I was angry. I was going to do more than shoot off a pinky toe. I was going to kill this bozo.

I continued to follow Leon and his woman that evening. They went from dinner to the casino and then I lost them when the valet handed Leon the keys to a fancy sports car. No doubt they were out for an evening of spending more and more of the money. I was so angry it took everything in me to keep from pulling out the gun.

# fourteen

I t was almost midnight when I returned to my hotel room, and to my surprise before I could peel off my clothes, the phone rang. No one knew I was here. I was hoping it wasn't hotel services telling me my credit card was no good. It wasn't. It was Powers.

"When you travel out of town to kill your husband you never use a credit card. It's a trail that proves you had opportunity." Powers' strong voice came through the earpiece.

I closed my eyes to the timbre of his voice. Why hadn't I married a man like this? A man who didn't steal, a man with integrity? "They told me I had to use a credit card." I sat down on the bed.

"If you'd told them you didn't have one, they would have taken cash. It's Vegas, Tamera."

"Then you wouldn't have been able to find me."

He chuckled. "I'm a detective. Credit card or no credit card, when I really want to, I can find anyone." I melted. I was in love. Really, I was or maybe I was so in hate with Leon, anyone was starting to sound good. I didn't want to talk about me. I didn't want to talk about Leon. I didn't want to talk about the money. I wanted to learn something about Kemuel Powers. Right this moment. I had his full attention, even if I was paying for it. I surmised that he was worth every dime.

"Tell me, my preaching detective, how was your sermon?"

"Great. I spoke to the youth about keeping their noses clean. About their destiny and their purpose. About not letting the devil and bad choices steal their futures."

I closed my eyes. I could hear the excitement in his voice. That message was all over me like a wet towel, but more than myself, it made me think of my brother. Todd needed to hear that sermon. He needed to hear it ten years ago. Powers was a power to be reckoned with. He was a super-power that God would use for good.

"Leon and I talked about raising kingdom kids. We were going to teach them all about destiny and purpose. In fact, our daughter's name was going to be Destiny. We were going to name our son, Joshua, because he would be a warrior. A real soldier for Christ." The memory saddened me so much, much more than seeing Leon and Delilah ever could.

"You'll do those same things. If that's what you want for your children, then God will bless you to have kingdom kids," Powers said. "You just have to find a real "king" to do it with."

"I don't know if there's anyone out there for me."

"Tamera, you are an intelligent, beautiful woman and your heart is so pure. Believe me, there's a man that's going to recognize that as the treasure it is. You just have to move past this stage in your life."

"If I'm so intelligent then how did I find Leon?"

"You didn't find him. He found you," Kemuel said. "He's a professional con artist. He preys on good people."

If he was here, I would have kissed him. God, those words sounded so good, so right. It felt like the Holy Spirit was speaking, trying to heal me. "Thanks, Kemuel." I'd never called him by his first name, but what he'd said was so personal and intimate that I felt like it was okay to do it.

I heard him let out a long sigh. "Why did you leave without me?"

I wanted to answer him, because of any number of reasons: I'm stupid, I don't think clearly, I'm a big fat loser, but he'd called me wonderful. I couldn't throw his compliment back in his face. "I don't know. I didn't want you involved. This is my mess. I – you're an evangelist and I have a gun."

"I have a gun."

"But you need one for your business. I have a gun because I'm contemplating shooting off a pinky toe."

Powers laughed a deep throaty sound that said I'd just helped him release a load of stress. "Can you even work that thing?"

"I had two – four hour lessons at Shooter's Galaxy. I'm a pro."

He laughed again and then his voice took on a serious tone. "Tamera, please come home. Let me help you handle this the right way."

"You said Leon was spending money like a fool. I've seen him. He is. He'll be broke by Friday. I—can't. I've got to at least try to reason with him. To get some of the money back."

"Tamera."

I closed my eyes to his plea, but I struggled with closing my heart. "I appreciate all you've done for me. I really do, but I've got to do this and I'm going to do it my way. I've come this far. A conversation with Leon isn't going to hurt."

"But you could get hurt. You may not be the only person with a gun."

"I have the element of surprise on my side. I promise. I won't let him hurt me. I have a plan."

We were silent for a long time. I knew Powers was thinking. He was trying to find the words to convince me that I was making a mistake. I also knew I was new at this. I knew this wasn't television. It wasn't a Hollywood movie like the Mr. and Mrs. Smith. I wasn't Angelina Jolie. But this was my life. This missing money was my problem. I had to solve it my way, so I wasn't going to be talked out of getting it.

"Wait for me." Powers begged. "Let's talk through the plan when I get there."

"No," I shook my head. "I'm breaking the law. Man's and God's. I don't want to involve you. I'll be home by early afternoon, and I promise I'll tell you all about it when I get there. Money or no money, okay?"

He was silent. It was not okay. "Wish me luck, or better yet, say a prayer for me. I know God is listening to you." I hung up the phone.

# fifteen

I t was eight o'clock in the morning. I knew those drinkin', partyin', spendin' ballers would definitely still be in bed. I knocked on the door three times before I finally heard a woman's voice on the other side. "Who the heck is it?"

"Hotel services ma'am." I disguised my voice.

"Yeah, well service something else. The do not disturb sign is up and it's eight –" I thought Delilah wasn't going to open up, but as she was complaining the door was opening.

As soon as I got a glimpse of the little tart, I pushed it hard, throwing Delilah's barely clothed form onto the floor. She screamed. I stepped in and pulled out the gun. "Shut up! Or I'll put a bullet in you."

Delilah sniffled and crawled back to the bed where Leon was sprawled out naked as the day he was born and knocked out cold. Seeing him like that sickened me and fueled my anger. I realized now wasn't the time to get emotional. I pointed the gun at Delilah. "On your feet tramp and wake that Negro up."

Delilah scampered to Leon's side and began to poke him in the head. "Leon, Leon, it's your wife."

"Oh, so you know who I am." Our eyes met and Delilah started sobbing. I fought the urge to shoot her.

Leon's eyes popped open. It took him a moment to come out of his sleepy haze, but when he did and he recognized me, shock and fear were all over his face. He cursed.

"I'm here for the money." I raised the gun to show him I meant business.

Leon pulled his body up on the bed and attempted to reach over the side of it.

"Don't move. I'll shoot."

"I'm just trying to get my drawers."

"I've seen your pitiful behind naked before. Remember, I'm your wife." There was a man's satin robe at the foot of the bed. I motioned toward it. "Give that to him."

Delilah's face was marred with a permanent grimace of fear. She looked like one of those distorted characters etched into the walls of the house of horrors at the amusement park. She followed my instructions and Leon attempted to cover himself like he thought I might shoot him in the family jewels. I smiled at the thought.

"Tammy, I— I—know you kind of mad wit me, but a gun. Wha—what—what – ch—ch -choo doing with a gun?"

Stuttering. What happened to his good diction? "I'm doing what you did. Robbing my spouse blind, honey. But I don't have five months to wine and dine you. I don't have time to listen to your sob stories or hear about your dreams. So I figured a semi-automatic handgun would get me what I wanted a whole lot faster."

"Leon." Delilah's breaths came heavy like she was having some kind of panic attack.

"Shut up, baby." Leon silenced her as he threw his legs over the side of the bed and stood. "Tam, you really need to stop pointing that gun at us. You don't know how to use that thing. You might hurt somebody."

"Not somebody." I stepped closer to the bed. "You."

Leon's hand trembled a bit. I could tell he was trying to think of something to say. "Now Tamera, I think we should be able to talk about this without that gun."

"Really?" I asked shaking my head. "I don't remember you talking to me before you stole my money."

Leon sighed.

"I would ask you the question most people ask in this situation. You know, how could you? But I had you checked out, Leon. Or is it Larry or Luther or Lex?" His eyes widened when I threw his aliases at him. "I won't ask, because I already know how you could. You're a thief and a con-artist and so is your bad weave wearing friend."

"Excuse me." Delilah rolled her neck.

I shook my head. "Save it sweetheart. The first thing you should have done when he gave you some money was fly to Atlanta and get yourself a decent piece of hair."

Delilah cut her eyes at me and raised her hand to pat the matted mess she'd obviously not tied up last night. She mumbled something under her breath, but I didn't hear it because my phone rang. I pulled it out of my jacket pocket and recognized Power's cell number. I ignored it. It began to ring again and then there was a loud knock on the door. I jumped. So did Leon and Delilah. "Who's that?" I asked.

They both shrugged like dumb and dumber. There was another knock and then a voice on the other side of the door that was faint, but discernable. "Tamera, it's me. Powers. Open up."

*No way.* I rolled my eyes upward and let out a long sigh. *No, he was not here. He had not come to Vegas.* I bit my lip. "Don't either one of you move, or I swear, I'll shoot and then you'll know I know how to use this thing." I slowly closed the distance between where I'd been and the door. I made sure to keep the gun trained on my captives while I turned the door knob with my free hand, but Leon leapt across the edge of the bed. He startled me so bad, I screamed and dropped the gun. The door flew open, and Powers entered the room. Seeing a half-naked Leon running in a silk robe must have turned on his cop instincts, because with lightening speed he charged at Leon, knocking him to the ground. I scrambled for the gun at my feet and picked it up. Powers gave me a disapproving look and got up off the floor. "Nice work."

"Thanks," I replied. "I was making progress. What are you doing here?"

"I came to help. I took the first flight I could get a seat on after we talked last night."

My stomach fluttered. He was rushing to my rescue. How sweet. No one had ever done that before.

"Hey," Leon barked getting up off the floor. "Who's he?" He sounded like a jealous husband.

"It's my partner in crime. Why should you get to have all the fun?" I twisted my lips into a shy smile and winked at Powers.

Leon returned to his spot against the wall with Delilah and I heard her whisper, "I thought you said she was stupid."

That got my attention. I moved closer to the bed. Trained the gun on Leon. "Stupid?"

"Dee, keep your friggin' mouth closed," Leon said, through grit teeth.

"Shut up!" I yelled. I raised the gun to Leon's chest. "Put your hands up." They did.

Powers took a few steps closer. "May I?" He questioned me with his eyes. I nodded. "Leon, your wife wants the money. She had a couple hours in a shooting range, but I'm not sure she's good enough to not accidentally fire off a round. The longer she holds that gun in her hand, the more likely she is to kill one of you," Powers said. "So, where is it?"

"I ain't answering you. I still don't even know who you are." Leon put his hands down and Delilah followed suit. "Tamera ain't 'bout to shoot nobody."

I reached into my pocket and pulled out the silencer. I had it on the gun so fast I surprised myself. I pointed the barrel down at the mattress, near Leon, and fired. Everybody in the room jumped including me. Leon began to pee. I pressed my lips together to keep from laughing.

"She could kill both of you and nobody would even hear it," Powers said.

Leon looked down at his wet leg and shook his head. "Lord have mercy, girl. It's in an account. I got the paperwork right here in the safe."

"Leon!" Delilah put her hands on her hips and shot daggers at him with her eyes. "What are you doing?"

"I ain't dying up in here over no money." Leon moved to the room safe and began to open it.

"Hold up," Powers said, stopping Leon. "I'll do that. What's the combination?"

Delilah was incensed. "What are you talking about? It's not just your money."

I couldn't believe this woman. I wanted to shoot her for having the nerve to think my money was now hers. "Shut up, trick!" I moved the gun in her direction. "These bullets ain't marital property."

Leon gave Powers the combination and Powers emptied the safe. "This is about five thousand dollars," he tossed a wad of cash on the bed. Then he pulled out Leon's precious prized jersey case and some paperwork that he scanned. He looked at me. "Fifty thousand dollars in an account in the Cayman Islands."

My heart sank. Fifty thousand of it wasn't even in the country. I dropped into a nearby chair. It never occurred to me that he'd send it off shore. Powers seemed to know what I was thinking. There was a lot of that between him and me. He picked up the five thousand and rushed to my side, kneeling. "This is good, Tamera. It makes things easier. We can just have him wire the money to your bank account."

I looked up at Leon who was rolling his eyes. Delilah had her arms crossed over her chest. She was leering at Leon, disgusted with him.

Powers stood. "Where's your laptop?"

Leon groaned.

# sixteen

Powers and Leon hovered around the laptop for a while. I provided the number for a credit union account I had through my job and within ten minutes of them completing the transaction I called and verified the funds were there. I put the five in my duffel bag. Fifty-five thousand dollars. Things were looking up, but not quite up enough. "I want the rest." The gun that had been at my side was now pointing at Leon again.

Leon shrugged his shoulders nonchalantly. "That's it. I got a Mercedes Coupe in the garage, this room and shoot, I done spent 'bout twenty thousand since we got here. He took a money clip off the table and tossed it to me. There's two thousand dollars." He went and pulled money out of Delilah's handbag. She hissed like a rattle snake. He tossed a wad of cash on the bed. "That's about a thousand."

Leon shrugged again. I smiled slyly. "You do think I'm stupid. I know you spent some, but there's money in a safe deposit account at New State Bank." Leon's eyes bugged wide. "Now, hubby, I want you to tie that tramp up and tape her mouth with this." I removed a roll of duct tape from my bag and tossed it on the bed. "Put your clothes on. We're going to get the rest of my money."

Delilah was all over him. "Leon, I know you not going to –"

"Dee, I done told you to shut up! What you want me to do, take a bullet so you can have the money?"

Delilah continued to rant. "I waited patiently while you was working this deal. If you give her—"

I was sick of the bickering back and forth. I put another bullet in the mattress. That got both their attention.

"Tamera, stop." I felt Powers strong hand on my shoulder. It traveled the length of my arm to the gun. I looked at him out of my peripheral vision. "The only way to get that money is to force him at gunpoint to the bank. You can't do that."

"Yes I can."

"No you can't."

"That fifty-eight thousand is not even enough to cover the corporate donations I have to return. And what about the money I spent finding him and my grandmother's house? I have a building. I have plans. I need the rest of it. I can't let them have the money from my grandmother's house."

"You also can't walk down the street holding a gun in his back." Powers took my free hand and turned me in Leon and Delilah's direction. "Really look at them. They aren't even worth it."

I broke down and started crying. He was right. I wanted the money so bad, I wasn't thinking. If Leon did one crazy thing on the street, I'd have to shoot him in public. I couldn't shoot him, in public or private. I wasn't a murderer. It would never work. I handed Powers the gun and he reached up and wiped the tears from my face with his thumb. "I'll tell you what we can do though." Powers careened his neck in Leon's direction. "We'll take the paperwork for that Mercedes," he paused, "and that Michael Jordan jersey."

Delilah let her body fall to the floor. "Leon!" Her whine was music to my ears.

Leon threw his arms up in disgust and started shaking his head. "Who is this dude?"

I grabbed Powers around the neck with so much force that I almost toppled him over. *Who was he?* "Super Powers," I whispered in his ear. I squeezed him tight and stepped back. "I would never have thought of the car."

Powers winked and flashed me a hundred watt smile. "I told you to wait for me."

# seventeen

I stood with the rest of the congregation and gave my girl a hardy hand clap for her rendition of "Is Your All On The Altar." Those voice lessons really paid off. She bought down the house and more importantly, she moved my spirit. I needed the message pastor preached today and I needed that song.

I milled around and spoke to some of the members as I waited. Everyone knew my plans for the Micah Center were on hold. They also knew my husband was gone and while there was some whispering, most were sympathetic and encouraging. "Hold on to God's unchanging hand. He'll make a way for that center to open." Words like that. They did my heart good.

Erin and the rest of the choir poured out of a back room. They were still giving my girl high fives and pats on the back. I was proud of her. She made her way to where I was standing. "I got an application for Sunday's Best in the car." I gave her a tight squeeze around the neck. "I felt like you sang that song just for me."

Erin waved a hand. "Girl, that was nothing. Just a little sumthin' sumpthin, because I still haven't shown y'all folks how talented a sistah is."

We laughed and walked out of the sanctuary.

"I have two-for-one coupons for brunch today. Linda is bringing her sister and T.S. is bringing a new diamond ring. She got engaged last night."

"Really," I said, thinking how nice for T.S. I couldn't help but think about how long I'd waited to find Mr. Right and now less than a year later I was right back where I started. Alone. "I'm going to have to miss the unveiling. I can't do brunch today."

Erin sunk visibly. "Come on. It's been forever since you joined us. I know you not still trying to hide your face. Don't nobody care about Leon."

I shook my head. "There's something I have to do. A little cleaning. I already made arrangements with Timothy House. They're coming to pick up the boxes in the morning."

Erin instantly knew what I meant. Timothy was a transitional house for homeless men who were getting back on their feet. "You want some help, girl?"

"No, this is something I have to do by myself. It's way overdue."

Erin gave me a tight squeeze. "I love you girl."

I squeezed back. "Love you too." I let her go and climbed into my car to pack up the last reminders of Leon Watson.


Leon's clothes filled six large cartons. My legs were tired from going up and down the stairs. I wished I could just throw it all out the back window and light a match, but the men in the Timothy House needed these clothes.

The stuff Leon left behind that was a curse to me, would be a blessing to them.

Once the closet was empty, I moved everything near the front door and went back upstairs to vacuum and dust. An hour later I was finished. My bedroom looked like it had before I gotten married, except for the unisex bedding and drapes. Maybe I would pull my lavender floral comforter set back out of storage and girly the place up again.

The doorbell rang. I bounced off the bed and jogged down the stairs. I wasn't expecting anyone and I'd taken to making sure to check at all times just in case Leon decided to pay me a visit, so I looked out the peep hole before I opened the door. My heart leapt.

"I was in the neighborhood. I thought I'd stop by and check on you." I moved back and allowed Powers to enter. He looked at the boxes suspiciously. "Moving?"

"Moving someone out." I smiled and we both stared at each other for a moment. My heart was racing a mile a minute. I was so glad to see him. "I have homemade lemonade. Would you like some?"

He nodded and followed me into the kitchen where I washed my hands and poured two glasses. We took seats at the table.

"How are you?"

I nodded. "I'm good. Really, really good."

"Have you heard from Leon?"

"Not a word. I'm sure he and Delilah have figured out some new scam. He's moved on. He won't bother me."

"I agree." Powers took a sip. "The alarm code for the house and the locks?"

"Changed." I took a deep breath. "I also filed for an annulment."

His eyes met mine and we held our gazes for awhile. "That's for the best. The sooner you're free of him, the sooner you can move on with your life."

"I haven't given up on my dream." I paused. "I'm still going to open the center one day. Thanks to you, I have almost twenty thousand dollars. I'm so glad you thought about the car or I'd still owe people money. I got the matching corporate monies once. I know I can get them again."

"I'm just glad you're okay."

Our eyes locked again and I realized I knew very little about this man that was making my heart thud. But I did know one very important thing. He'd helped me get my life back, helped me save my dignity and that was worth more than any amount of money.

"I'm also glad to hear you're not giving up, because I actually have some good news." Powers removed an envelope from his pocket.

I raised my eyebrows. "I could use good news. What is it?"

"Well, you know I was digging around in Leon's past. It turns out he has money in an unclaimed fund that he apparently doesn't know anything about."

I sat up straighter. "Are you kidding?"

"He had a great aunt that died more than ten years ago in Mississippi. She owned a house. It wasn't worth much. The value of it had been depreciating every year. The county tore it down to build a school and put the money from the settlement offer in unclaimed funds. Guess who her only living heir is?"

I shook my head and chuckled. "No way."

Powers nodded. "It's almost fifteen thousand dollars. Once the civil claim against Leon is filed, you can put a lien on that money. He doesn't even know about it to fight it." Powers slid the envelope to me. I reached for it and my fingers grazed his. The tingle was so electric it sent a shock through my entire body. Powers must have felt it too, because he reached for my hand and intertwined his fingers with mine. "So you still have a little over twenty thousand, this fifteen and I've been thinking. I'd like to invest in a dream." His mouth broke into that incredibly sexy, crooked, smile I'd come to love.

"You are such a superpower," I whispered. We met each other halfway across the table and finally kissed.

# About the Authors

Author **Tiffany L. Warren** is the author of the national bestselling novel, *In The Midst of It All* (Feb 2010) and the highly acclaimed novels *The Bishop's Daughter* (Jan 2009) *Farther Than I Meant To Go, Longer Than I Meant To Stay* (Oct 2006) and *What A Sista Should Do* (June 2005). Tiffany also writes young adult novels under the pen name Nikki Carter and is the visionary of the annual Faith and Fiction Retreat for faith based authors and readers. Tiffany is a wife and mother of five children. She and her family reside in Houston, Texas. You may learn more about her at her website www.tiffanylwarren.com

**Sherri Lewis** is the *Essence* Bestselling author of *The List* (March 2009), *My Soul Cries Out* (July 2007), *Dance Into Destiny* (Jan 2008) and the highly anticipated sequel to My Soul Cries Out, *Selling My Soul* (March 2010). Sherri's life passion is to express the reality of the Kingdom of God through the arts including music, dance, films and television and literature; and through sound biblical teaching. Her ministry thrusts include the message of the Kingdome, intimacy with God, intercessory prayer, understanding prophetic ministry, ministering emotional healing, and birthing individuals into their destiny. She lives in Atlanta, Georgia. You may learn more about Sherri and her novels at www.sherrilewis.com

**Rhonda McKnight** is the author of the *Black Expressions* Bestselling novel, *Secrets and Lies* (Dec 2009) and *An Inconvenient Friend* (coming August 1, 2010). She is also the owner of *Legacy Editing*, a free-lance fiction editing service and *Urban Christian Fiction Today*, a popular Internet site that highlights African-American Christian Fiction. Rhonda is the mother of two sons she prophetically calls her "Soldiers for Christ". Originally from a small coastal town in New Jersey, she's called Atlanta, Georgia home for twelve years. You may learn more about Rhonda and her novels at her website www.rhondamcknight.net

# Books by Tiffany L Warren

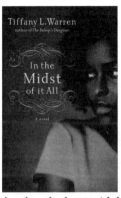

### *In The Midst of It All*
February 2010

All her life, Zenovia has struggled with the burden of caring for her schizophrenic mother, Audrey, alone. Until one day, God seems to offer support in the form of two members of a church called the Brethren of the Sacrifice, who knock at the women's door preaching an unconventional version of the Gospel. Despite having questions, Zenovia agrees to join the church along with her mother.

Soon afterward, Audrey stops taking her medication when fellow churchgoers deem her illness a demonic possession. Unable to watch her mother's mental deterioration, Zenovia flees town, only to receive a fateful phone call several years later telling her of her mother's suicide. Heartbroken, Zenovia must now make a soul-altering choice: accept "God's will," or return home to confront the demons she's worked so hard to leave behind....

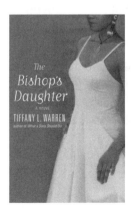

### *The Bishop's Daughter*
January 2009

Darrin Bainbridge is your typical playboy in need of love, but not yet ready. He is a freelance journalist trying to break his big story. After a visit from his mother, Darrin gets an idea. He has heard all kinds of stories about "Hollywood" ministers who hold their church services on television, live in nice houses, drive nice cars, and have lots of money and women. Darrin is disgusted by it all especially when his mother Priscilla starts shouting praises for Atlanta Bishop Kumal Prentiss. Darrin decides to go to Atlanta, become a member of the bishop's church, and expose him for the hustling fraud that he believes he is. He just never planned on falling in love with the Bishop's daughter. Darrin suddenly finds himself torn between his new found friend and his possible big break.

### *Farther than I Meant to Go, Longer than I Meant to Stay*
November 2006

As President of Grace Savings and Loans, Charmayne Ellis is an established, polished professional. Although she has reached great success, her ridiculing mother and wise cracking younger sister won't let her forget that she is a 36-year-old, overweight, unmarried woman.

In an attempt to help, Charmayne's best friend, Lynette, is obsessed with setting her up on a series of pity-driven blind dates. When a drop-dead gorgeous man, Travis Moon, shows interest, Charmayne's caution light blinks like crazy. But out of loneliness and pressure from her family Charmayne ignores her gut feeling and gets married.

Yet instead of marital bliss, Charmayne begins to discover new things about her husband that force her to question her marriage and her faith in God.

## *What a Sista Should Do*
June 2005

Pam Lyons has a husband who places more trust in money and marijuana than in God. Yvonne Hastings is a minister's wife whose husband's infidelity and physical abuse brings their marriage to a crossroads. Taylor Johnson is a single mother who is looking for a good Christian man to help raise her son, but is unable to rid herself of the guilt left over from her promiscuous past. The secret of Taylor's child's paternity is the catalyst for the tumultuous relationship between the three women. Together, they will learn unforgettable lessons about love, forgiveness, prayer, and sisterhood.

**www.tiffanylwarren.com**

**www.faithandfictionretreat.com**

# Books by Sherri L. Lewis

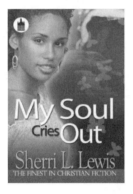

### *My* Soul *Cries Out*

July 2007

Monica Harris Day's perfect world begins a downward spiral when she comes home to find her husband in bed with another man. This novel is a compassionate look at Christians struggling with homosexuality and the power of God to bring deliverance.

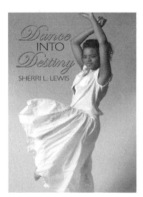

### *Dance Into Destiny*

January 2008

A novel about the purpose driven life...

A purpose socialite and a purpose driven church mouse form an unlikely friendship and become God-chasers on a journey of destiny and purpose.

### *The List*
March 2009

3 single, successful, saved-but-still-sexy are tired of waiting on God to bring their soul mates. They make a list of everything they want in a man and go on a hilarious dating adventure trying to be found by their husbands.

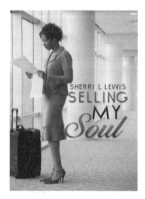

### *Selling My Soul*
March 2010

Trina Michaels returns from her African mission trip to her career in public relations. When she's forced to do damage control for a Bishop whose church is involved in a sex scandal, she risks losing her best friend, her new love, and is in danger of selling her soul.

## Read all the 1st chapters at
## www.sherrilewis.com

# Books by Rhonda McKnight

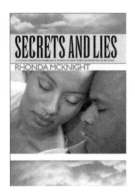

### *Secrets and Lies*
Dec 2009

Faith Morgan is struggling with her faith. Years of neglect leave her doubting that God will ever fix her marriage. When a coworker accuses her husband, Jonah, of the unthinkable, Faith begins to wonder if she really knows him at all, and if it's truly in God's will for them to stay married.

Pediatric cardiologist Jonah Morgan is obsessed with one thing: his work. A childhood incident cemented his desire to heal children at any cost, even his family, but now he finds himself at a crossroads in his life. Will he continue to allow the past to haunt him, or find healing and peace in a God he shut out long ago?

### *An Inconvenient Friend*
Aug 2010

Samaria Jacobs has her sights set on Gregory Preston. A successful surgeon, he has just the bankroll she needs to keep her in the lifestyle that her credit card debt has helped her grow accustomed to. Samaria joins New Mercies Christian Church to get close to Gregory's wife. If she gets to know Angelina Preston, she can become like her in more than just looks, and really work her way into Greg's heart.

Angelina Preston's life is filled with a successful career and busy ministry work, but something's just not right with her marriage. Late nights, early meetings, lipstick- and perfume-stained shirts have her suspicious that Greg is doing a little more operating than she'd like. But does she have the strength to confront the only man she's ever loved and risk losing him to the other woman? Just when Samaria thinks she's got it all figured out, she finds herself drawn to Angelina's kindness. Will she be able to carry out her plan after she finds herself yearning for the one thing she's never had . . . the friendship of a woman?

**www.rhondamcknight.net**

**www.facebook.com/booksbyrhonda**